Minus 55

by

Andrew Odom

**Dry Bones Press
San Francisco, CA 94164**

Minus 55

By Andrew Odom

Copyright 1999, 2000, Andrew Odom

Photography: Mark Slankard
Model: Jim Herrell

Dry Bones Press, Inc.
P. O. Box 640345
San Francisco, CA 94164
(415) 707-2129

http://www.drybones.com/

Publishers Cataloging-in-Publication Data
Odom, Andrew, 1974—
Minus 55 / by Andrew Odom
    New Voices in American Fiction: Science Fiction
    & Fantasy Series
p.   cm.
ISBN 1-883938-42-2
Fiction. / Science Fiction & Fantasy
I. Author II. Title III. Series

For my family.

ODOM

Contents:

1. Minus 55 5

2. Figments, Inc. 25

3. Internal Combustion 45

4. The New Scent 62

5. Strange Assistants 79

6. B.A.D. 104

7. Slow Sedation 114

8. A Lobotomy and a Chest X-ray ... 121

9. Lights Out 130

10. The Bionic Hand 133

11. New Reality 136

12. Roulette 156

13. **Minus 56** **163**

"Minus 55"

Part One

Jack sat alone, he and a half–empty bottle of whiskey, and waited for the big midnight celebration to begin. He was dressed in his usual work outfit—a white jumpsuit with stars and stripes up and down the sides and sleeves, stretched over his body. Red and white stripes, yellow stars.

The room Jack was in was some kind of storage deal with cardboard boxes and stripped wires laying around. The dusty smell of bygone physical labor hung in the air. It wasn't much, he thought, but at least it was more interesting now than when he'd come in—back when the bottle had been full.

Beyond the door Jack could hear loud music, joyous music, filling the dining hall where he was to perform. He could hear all the people acting happy. He imagined the clinking of champagne glasses and the chit–chat, could already smell the expensive perfumes and colognes. He could feel all the handshakin' and networkin'. Nothing specific, just the general mass of the festive beast waiting for the freak to entertain it.

The occasion was New Year's Eve—every year, just like clockwork—and Jack drank to that. The building was the headquarters of The National Broadcasting Company and the people awaiting his entertainment were the minions who kept the conglomerate at the top. Jack drank to them all.

"Fifteen minutes, Mr. Simmons," said a stage manager, popping his wired–up head into the room. And he was quickly gone, shutting the door behind him.

"Don't call me mister, you son–of–a–bitch," Jack yelled at the door, slapping his hand against the tabletop. Then he laughed and drank to the stage manager.

ODOM

It had been fourteen years, almost to the day, since Jack had been in this building. It seemed different to him now, smaller than it had back when he was getting his big chance. He had sat in the office of a company executive, Travis Boone, an old friend of his agent's, and ironed out a deal that he believed would land him center stage at the most watched awards show in the world. It was to be the biggest, most publicized escape in the history of publicized escapes. It was going to be sensationally dangerous. It was going to make Jack a star—a hero to the masses.

Up to that point, Simmons had done everything right—played his cards perfectly. He'd nailed every escape, kept himself pretty and overtly available to the ladies, and he'd done every interview that came his way. He was red silk, ready to shine in the neon lights of Hollywood or thereabouts, ready to have books written about him, ready to be loved or loathed by everyone.

But it all fell through. Boone was arrested, indicted, and convicted for having had his wife killed. It was big news, even for The National Broadcasting Company, the biggest entertainment conglomerate in the world. Subsequently, Jack, along with all of Boone's other ideas and plans, were no longer a part of NBC. The broadcast giant washed its hands of the whole mess and, as Jack saw it, stole from him the one opportunity he needed—his big moment at the big show. Another shot never came around.

And all because someone else blew it.

A man came through the door. "How ya doin', Jack–o?" said the man —Buddy Friend, Jack's agent and self–proclaimed master of self–promotion. He was wearing one of his white suits and wide, red ties. His mustache glistened in the storage room light.

"I'm hangin' in. How you doin'? You holdin' up OK?

MINUS 55

Seemed a little nervous earlier."

Buddy sat down at the table, wiped his upper lip with a handkerchief and exhaled a long breath. He smiled and shook his head, crossed his legs and lined up the crease of his pants with the center of his knee. His hair was tumbleweed, black and grey, dying from too many years of being made presentable.

"This has been a real rigmarole," Buddy said. "From the beginning. I think I can finally relax a little. I think everything's gonna take care of itself now, you know what I mean? I'm kinda glad it's out of my hands." He spoke like one of those guys that gangsters kill in the movies.

Jack slid the bottle of whiskey across the table toward his agent and friend, and then the glass after it. Friend poured himself a drink and knocked it back. "Thanks," he said.

"Have as much as you want," said Jack. "I think I'm just about where I need to be."

Friend played with the glass, held it between his fingers and swirled what was left of his first drink around in the bottom. He pulled a pack of cigarettes out of the pocket inside his coat and a lighter out of his pants pocket, lit a smoke. "So what'd you do today to get ready for the big event?" he asked.

Jack slid a little further down into his seat. "Went down and caught one of them shitty films that's showin' at the omniplex."

Buddy smiled. "Which one did you have the misfortune of catchin'?"

"Ahhh…" Jack waved his hands around trying to jar loose a thought. "…one of them end–of–the–world, asteroid pictures. You've probably seen the ads for 'em, haven't ya? They're all over the damn place."

"Yeah, they got that billboard for the one right outside a here, right?"

ODOM

"Yeah," Jack answered, pointed to where the billboard would be if they could see through walls.
"You go by yourself?" Buddy asked.
"Nah, took Sarah with me."
"Really? Sarah leadin' the pack, is she?"
"She's the blossom flower amongst the weeds."
Buddy laughed. "Are you weedin' her out?"
Jack smiled. "Yeah, weedin' her out."
Buddy threw his head back and let a cloud of smoke drift out of his mouth. "And the movie wasn't any good? It had one of them happy movie endings?"
Jack leaned forward and reached across the table for Buddy's pack of cigarettes. "I'm not even sure, really. We walked out just when it looked like everybody was gonna eat the big asteroid. Kinda created our own little ending. Made it better that way, I think." Jack pulled a cigarette out of the pack and stuck it between his lips. "I think I oughta be editing these films." He asked for the lighter and Buddy hesitated, then gave in without an argument.
"Abraham Lincoln," Jack said, checking the picture on the front of the lighter.
"The Great Emancipator," said Buddy. He poured another drink for himself and knocked it back. He checked his watch. "We've got about ten minutes before they come in and get you. You say you're ready, huh?" he said, knocked another drink.
"I probably need to take a piss. I don't want to be squeezin' my thighs together when that goddamned water hits me."
Buddy smiled. "I like that. That's bein' professional."
Jack agreed and then stood up, straight as an arrow, his jumpsuit bowing away from his chest where the zipper was undone. He smiled at how steady he could stand, winked at Buddy

and then headed to the bathroom, through the door to his left—the one with white paint strips dangling off the front of it, exposing the wood. The unshaded light in the small bathroom hit Jack's eyes hard and made him wobble once the door was shut tightly behind him. He took a moment to adjust himself to the white sterility of the room—which he figured to be a lie—and to the cold breeze that seemed to be coming from somewhere imperceptible. He unzipped his suit down his right leg and a chill ran through him thoroughly, up and down his spine a couple times. It made him feel clean. The whiskey was all about him now, too. He felt the brown warmth of a whiskey drunkenness and felt the worry and anxiety of the night's imminent performance being pulled from his shoulders like a wet undershirt.

He made his way to the dusty toilet. The black swimming briefs beneath his jumpsuit were tight but very elastic and he freed himself easily and started to drain the transparent piss from his body. He propped himself up with his left hand on the rough, concrete wall in front of him, steadied things with his right. He pushed it hard and it was loud in the bowl, like two people pissin'. It made him smile.

After Jack finished, he finished a few times more and flushed the toilet. Then he stood for a moment in front of the dirty mirror above the sink. He leaned in closely and pressed his nose against the cold surface, breathing moisture onto it from his mouth and nose. He watched his pupils go in and out, on and off. He wondered why all of him was still working.

He backed away and looked at his body—pulled the jumpsuit down over his shoulders, exposing his chest. It wasn't as pretty as it once was, but it was alright. He arched his head back and drew long breaths in through his nose and then let them out through his mouth. He rubbed his hand over his chest and smiled. Jack was feeling good, better than he had in a long time.

ODOM

The party music seemed louder in the bathroom—maybe just because the party was steadily careening toward the striking of the New Year. He listened for a moment for anything important, but all he could hear was Buddy talking to him through the bathroom door.

"Get yourself back in here, Jack. Let me go over this with you one more time."

Jack took a last look at his body and then one at his eyes. He washed his mouth out in the sink and adjusted his swimming briefs to maximize his comfort level—pushed the whole package toward the left side. Then he zipped up and went back to his friend and his whiskey.

# # #

"OK. They're gonna lead you out to the stage about seven minutes—actually, seven minutes on the nose—before midnight," Buddy said.

Jack took his seat. "Who?"

"A stage manager'll take you to the backstage apron and then the MC's gonna introduce you, give you the big entrance and everything, and then you'll come out."

"The tank'll be out there, filled up and everything? How 'bout them shackles and all that?" Jack asked.

"Don't you worry about all of that. That'll be taken care of, already has been. You just make sure you wave to the crowd. Have a goddamn smile on your face for Chrissakes. All that little shit's gonna take care of itself."

Jack drained the last bit of whiskey out of the bottle and into his mouth and sat it back on the table. "I'll take care of everything, Buddy. Don't worry yourself about it."

"Do you know all of the time requirements, all of that?"

"Yeah, but go over 'em again just to make sure."

Buddy stood up from his chair and went to the door. He

10

cracked it open enough to take a look around the hallway. He let the sounds in, let them bounce around the room real good so Jack could get his blood pumping.

"OK. The only thing you really have to remember is that you're supposed to be in that tank for no longer than two minutes. You have to get out in plenty of time to help with the New Year's countdown."

"Two minutes. If I'm in there so much as a minute and a half you can be certain I've inhaled enough water to kill three or four of me."

Buddy didn't respond.

"So they're gonna put me in the tank about four minutes 'til midnight, right?"

"Yeah," Buddy answered, "you'll go behind the screen between three–and–a–half minutes till and four minutes till."

"Pretty precise."

"Yeah." Buddy paced circles around the room, around Jack and his table. He was nervous—far more than so than Jack. "This is the big one, Jack," he said. "Don't you think it's the big one?"

Jack was silent. Buddy walked and wrung his hands.

"It's been, what, fourteen years. And now they're giving you a second chance. It's not every day that a man gets a second chance."

"That's bullshit and you know it's bullshit," Jack said and laughed. "If you remember right, there never was a first chance." He picked up the empty bottle and spun it around in his hand. "Hey," he said. "Forget about it. Those people out there are gonna remember this night, tonight, Buddy. Those people are gonna remember who the hell 'Suicide' Simmons is."

# # #

Jack and Buddy sat and waited the last minutes before

ODOM

being escorted to the stage area. It was silent in the room except for the party sounds bleeding in through the cracks around the door. Buddy tapped his nervous fingers on the table. Jack slouched down in his chair, hands behind his head, and spread his legs out in front of him.

All this waiting reminded Jack of the handful of trips he'd taken to the doctor when he'd been a kid. Sitting in the waiting room, waiting for your turn to be called in—told whether you were broken or not. He'd broken his left arm three times, never anything else, and he examined the wing as he and Buddy waited—compared it to his right—in order to kill some time. It wasn't any different, but it seemed like it ought to be.

The door to the storage room opened and the wired head reappeared.

"Ready?" asked the wired head.

"That tank full?" Jack asked, leaning forward as if he was going to spring forth and attack the wired head.

"Everything's taken care of Mr. Simmons."

Jack slapped the table again, said "woo," and knocked the empty bottle onto its side where it rolled back and forth in a semi–circle. The stage manager laughed a little, tapped his fingers on his clipboard.

"Yeah, we're ready," said Buddy and he and Jack stood up and straightened out their suits—Buddy his red tie, Jack his zipper, allowing just enough of his chest to show.

"OK, guys. Let's go ahead and get you out there," said the stage manager, holding the door open for the two men.

The hallway was dark after the door to the waiting room was closed and, although there were lights above them, it seemed as if it was only bright up ahead. It seemed to stay dark, the antisocial light scattering away from them as they walked. The crowd noise got louder, and the music swelled although it remained unintelligible. Just a mass of noise with no reason or rhythm.

"This is going to be great, huh," the stage manager said. "We've been looking forward to this all day."

"Yes, yes," said Buddy. "This'll be something. It should be the big event of the night."

They turned a corner, took a right, and in the distance could see the words "Stage 1" painted on the wall in front of them. Next to the words was an arrow, large and red, pointing to the left, through a large set of double doors. The noise was coming from there.

"This is the backstage, here. We've still got several minutes..." The stage manager checked his watch. "...five minutes or so before they call you out. You can get used to the surroundings, check out the stage, check out the equipment, whatever you need to do. We realize you've already gone over things earlier, but if you want to go over things again in the next few minutes, go right ahead. You've got time if you wanna go over things and check things out a little bit...If you wanna do that, it'll be no problem. You've got the time and all of that...a little time anyhow."

Jack cracked his knuckles, cracked his elbow joints, his wrists, and then snapped his neck around to pop it, too. He stopped in front of the double doors, took down his zipper a couple more notches and turned his red collar up behind his neck.

"I'm ready," he said.

The doors swung open into the backstage area. It was big and dark, cables hanging from every which place. People were walking around with their headsets and clipboards—some were in suits and some were dirty. All of them looked at Jack when he made his entrance. He'd have had it no other way. He longed to drink to each and every one of them.

ODOM

"Pretty big stuff, hey Jack–o," said Buddy.
"Pretty big," Jack agreed.

The stage manager walked to the side of the stage, to the steps behind the curtain, about twenty five feet from the light of the stage. He called Jack and Buddy over to him and showed them the tank, which was surrounded by another curtain, a red one, obscuring it from the crowd in a brilliant, satin semi–circle. He also showed Jack the chest full of shackles that were to be used and Jack quickly gave them a once–over. He then looked back to the tank that was standing next to a wide platform that rose at least eight feet off the stage.

From Jack's perspective during the show, the tank would be immediately to the right of the platform. It was big and gold with red satin reflecting off it. It was one of the nicest things Jack had ever seen. The water was dark, not much light falling onto it because of the semi–circle, and it was still.

Jack took a deep breath and exhaled through his mouth so he could smell the whiskey. He was anxious to get out there under those lights. Everything was going perfectly. He only wished he could see the expression on the audience's face.

A man brushed between Jack and Buddy on his way to the stage steps—a man in an expensive suit, a tiny card in his hand, and a smile that could sell the world.

"HI, I'M ARMAND LYLE, THE MC," the man said, turning toward Jack, extending his right hand. "I'LL BE THE ONE INTRODUCING YOU TONIGHT."

Jack shook the hand and then Buddy did the same.

"WELL, BREAK A LEG," said the MC.

"You bet," Jack said and then turned to Buddy as Mr. Lyle made his way up the steps and toward the break in the curtain. "He didn't have any whiskey on *his* breath."

"Yeah," Buddy said. "He makes enough to afford the shit

that doesn't stink."

The MC emerged from the side of the stage, Jack assumed, when he heard a change in the crowd noise. The party music stopped and a hush fell over the audience. Now, everybody in the backstage area took their positions—some of them were looking out toward the lights, past the background curtain on stage, and some were busy at their stations, the stations required for pulling the whole evening together.

"Ready?" the stage manager said. He'd slipped off for a minute or so, going over some things with another guy wearing similar equipment and carrying a clipboard.

"Yeah."

"OK. Now, Mr. Friend, you go on out when Jack's announced. Mr. Lang'll introduce you both when you guys get out there."

"Great," Buddy said.

"Then they'll bring up the three people from the crowd—the CEO's daughter, the president's wife, and whoever else."

"Six of us up there?" Jack asked.

"Yeah. Plus two stagehands, but they'll be out of the way."

From in front of the curtain, the MC, Armand Lyle, started in with his big voice: "ALL RIGHT LADIES AND GENTLEMEN. IT'S ONLY A FEW MORE MINUTES TO THE NEW YEAR. [Applause] BUT FIRST...LET US WELCOME...THE GREATEST LIVING ESCAPIST IN ALL THE WORLD..."

# # #

The stage lights were hotter than Jack had expected and he heard the audience as though he was already underwater. He could feel the energy of the event coming at him from every direction. Had Jack needed it, that energy could have held him upright.

He felt more inebriated once he took the stage. The feed-

ODOM

back from the audience and the lights and the MC's big, famous, booming voice came at him in waves. That water was gonna to feel real good, he thought. Inside the tank would be some real electricity, a good place for him to concentrate on his business.

The volunteers were called up to the stage after the MC had introduced both Jack and Buddy to the applauding crowd. The CEO's daughter, the first to be "picked," looked to be in her twenties, but was dressed up like she was older. The president's wife, the second pick, was probably fifty or so—dressing herself down to about forty, perhaps—and lookin' good. The third person, the actual volunteer of the bunch, was a great big guy—all muscled up and coming through his dinner jacket. It looked like his tie was going to cut into his neck or burst into strands against the bulging veins that pumped his machismo.

Jack was glad he was up there, volunteer #3. It always helped to have a big motherfucker around to pull and tug on all the chains and shackles, all the machinery of the escape. It made the whole enterprise look legit. Which, of course, it was. It was as legitimate as it could be without being suicide—just a notch under suicide.

Everybody was on the platform now, to the left and just above the tank. The volunteers were all smiles as were Buddy and the MC. Jack, however, was point–blank—no smile, no expression at all. He stared into the sea of suits and ties and dresses, into all that money. Part of him wanted to laugh at them and let loose his vulgarity on them, but it didn't.

"OK THERE, JACK. GET YOURSELF READY," the MC said.

Jack unzipped his jumpsuit slowly, all the way down to his right knee. The heat from the lights and the pre–event whiskey helped to keep him from becoming chilled. He slowly let the shoulders drop down around his waist and then slithered out the

MINUS 55

rest of the way. There he was, standing atop a platform that stood a good eight feet off the floor of a stage. Flash bulbs flashed and there was some chatter. Jack knew he didn't look great nine-tenths of the way naked, but he hoped that the places of flab and discoloration would only enhance his final performance.

"AT LEAST WE KNOW HE'S NOT SHY, HEY FOLKS!" the MC belted and the crowd laughed and relaxed in the presence of the flesh.

Jack looked at the MC and grinned slightly, he winked at the CEO's daughter. When the crowd quieted, the MC continued the presentation.

"OUR STAGE HANDS WILL NOW SHACKLE MR. SIMMONS—ONE RESTRAINT AROUND EACH WRIST, ONE ABOUT EACH ANKLE, AND ONE ABOUT BOTH THE WAIST AND THE NECK. THIS IS A VERY DANGEROUS ESCAPE INDEED. ONE THAT WILL, MOST ASSUREDLY, GO DOWN AS ONE OF THE FINEST IN ALL OF HISTORY..."

As the MC rambled on about bravery and danger, the stagehands worked quickly with the locks. The taller man, taller than Jack, snapped the neck manacle into place, tight around Jack's neck. Then he shackled the wrists with irons, clicking them firmly into place. In the meantime, the shorter stagehand, a younger-looking man, put leg irons around Jack's ankles and snapped them shut. He then pulled tight a thick chain around Jack's waist and locked it in as well.

The steel was cold against Jack's skin. The neck chain was too high and he had to work it down over his Adam's apple in order to breathe easily. He popped his neck down and in and back out again, working the steel down so he didn't choke.

"AND NOW WE'LL LET OUR VOLUNTEERS INSPECT THE SHACKLES AND CHAINS."

They were lined up, the three of them right there on the

stage next to Jack, and they all took their turn pressing and pulling and manipulating. Nothing budged.

The volunteers were backed off and Jack looked into the crowd again as the MC was explaining the next step. He could see their anticipation. He could feel a tension building.

The MC continued: "AND NOW JACK WILL STEP ABOARD THE PLATFORM THAT IS ABOVE THE WATER CHAMBER. AS THE VOLUNTEERS CAN SEE, ATOP THE PLATFORM—LOCATED AT THE FRONT, FACING YOU, THE AUDIENCE—ARE SIX AREAS WHERE CHAINS OF VARYING LENGTHS HAVE BEEN ATTACHED.

The volunteers took a few moments to look over the top of the platform and then indicate to the crowd the truth of those chain locations.

"AND NOW...JACK WILL STEP ABOARD THE PLATFORM."

Jack stepped onto the platform. He could feel impressions forming on the bottoms of his feet from the holes in the platform bottom—the ones that would eventually let water pass through them upon submersion. The platform was sturdy, but swayed just a bit over the tank as Jack shifted on his feet.

"TO THE SIX CHAINS JACK WILL BE FASTENED. ONE CHAIN FROM THE PLATFORM TO HIS NECK. ONE CHAIN FROM THE PLATFORM TO HIS RIGHT WRIST AND ONE TO HIS LEFT. ONE CHAIN FROM THE PLATFORM TO HIS WAIST AND THE TWO REMAINING CHAINS, THE SHORTEST CHAINS, FROM THE PLATFORM TO HIS ANKLES."

The stagehands snapped and clicked the restraining chains into place and pulled on them to attest to their snugness. Then the volunteers were allowed to so the same.

The ladies were quickly satisfied, but The Muscle seemed

intent on making sure of things. He pulled hard on the chains in all directions. Occasionally, he even hurt Jack. But that was OK. He was only helping to build the legend. Eventually, Muscles backed off and offered a thumbs up to the crowd. They responded with loud applause, only falling silent again as the MC raised his hands.

Jack turned his head what little he could and looked at Buddy. He was stern–looking. Jack could see "Don't fuck this up," written all over his face.

Looking down through the holes in the octagon and into the water, Jack could see that it was no longer calm down there, not entirely. The water was slapping softly against the sides of the tank as Jack swayed above it. He had an itch under his nose, but couldn't raise his chained hands above his waist. When he strained against the chains, the itch went away. It was a good thing for the crowd to see.

"AND NOW, JACK WILL BE SUBMERGED INSIDE AN EIGHT FOOT COLUMN OF WATER, CHAINED TO THE BOTTOM, WITH NO MORE THAN A COUPLE MINUTES OF AIR IN HIS LUNGS. BEHIND THE SCREEN—USED TO PROTECT MR. SIMMONS' ARTISTRY—JACK MUST FREE HIMSELF OF ALL SIX CHAINS AND THEN THROW OPEN THE STEEL LID THAT WILL BE SLAMMED SHUT OVER THE TOP OF HIM. AND IF HE DOES NOT!"

The audience groaned.

"ARE YOU WITH HIM!" the MC roared and the audience roared right back at him.

Jack looked out into the audience again. He was pleased to see so many faces and hear so many of them screaming and yelling. And after fourteen years, it was finally time, time for the show.

ODOM

Part Two

Little Sarah sat at a table in the second row of the dining hall. She was close enough to the stage to feel the energy. She was close enough to really *see* Jack. To her, Jack was impressive, a genius of sorts. He'd done everything, seen everything.

Sarah sat with her legs dangling off the front of her seat. She was a little uncomfortable with that dress on—the pink and red one her mother had picked out for her—and she kept sliding, slowly forward, toward the edge of her brightly polished seat.

Her father sat next to her—to her left. But all she could see of him was his tuxedoed back, as his front was talking to one of the men Sarah had heard him refer to as an "associate," whatever that was. Her mother was talking to one of her "girlfriends."

Why boys didn't call their friends "boyfriends," Sarah couldn't figure. Boys are silly, Sarah thought.

But not Jack. Jack wasn't silly. He was the real thing. Sarah couldn't understand why her father and mother weren't paying more attention—why they were so involved with those other people—when Jack was the one to be giving your attention to.

As the MC spoke and the stagehands shackled and the volunteers checked and pulled, the butterflies swarmed in little Sarah's stomach. Jack was above the tank now, above the cold water. He was dressed like Tarzan.

Sarah could see the slight uneasiness of the platform Jack stood upon. She could see Jack shift his weight from one foot to another, balancing the whole act above that frigid water. She saw him strain against the chains to scratch at his face and part of her felt sympathy for him—like he was helpless.

The MC spoke: "...JACK MUST FREE HIMSELF OF ALL SIX CHAINS AND THEN THROW OPEN THE STEEL

LID THAT WILL BE SLAMMED OVER THE TOP OF HIM. AND IF HE DOES NOT..."

The audience groaned.

"ARE YOU WITH HIM!"

The audience roared.

Sarah's parents did not. They were saying things like "business" and "money," "so pretty" and "credit card," laughing and drinking.

There was a drumroll from somewhere off–stage. There must be a drummer behind the curtain, Sarah thought. A whole group of musicians, perhaps.

The MC raised a shiny box into the air with his right hand, a box that had an antenna extending from the end of it. It looked like the future. The crowd became focused and Sarah heard her father say "Well, I guess we're supposed to watch this." He and Sarah's mother were now in the game.

The drumroll grew louder, soaring upward and keeping rapid tempo, keeping time with Sarah's butterflies.

The MC spoke: "I WILL NOW START THE DESCENT OF THE PLATFORM. ARE YOU READY, GENTLEMEN?"

The stagehands nodded their heads. They were kneeling beside Jack, holding the heavy, steel lid in their hands.

"IS THE AUDIENCE READY?"

They were ready.

"ARE YOU READY, JACK?"

Jack nodded, cool as hanging meat.

"GOOD LUCK, MR. SIMMONS. WE'LL SEE YOU IN A COUPLE OF MINUTES."

The MC brought the shiny box down in front of his chest and brought his other hand out there with it. He pressed its big, red button and the platform bounced once and began its steady drop into the tank.

ODOM

Sarah imagined how cold that water must have been, rising up over Jack's ankles, steadily taking in more and more of him. She wondered how long Jack could hold his breath. As the water overcame his waist, Sarah's butterflies stopped to watch the action. She felt a heaviness in her stomach.

The shield for the tank was put into place, blocking the front of the tank from the audience. There were some disappointed groans scattered throughout the mass, but Sarah didn't really care about seeing what was happening under that water. She knew it was magic. And she knew that you don't have to see magic for there to be magic. When the chain around Jack's neck disappeared behind the red velvet shield, as eventually did his mouth, Sarah took the deepest breath she could take and held onto it.

When Jack was gone, the stagehands slammed the lid shut and stood away from the rest of the people on the stage—behind them all. A big clock above the tank and platform showed a countdown from two minutes—as did another from the left side, near the pulled back curtain—and everyone in the gallery became silent. In what seemed like half the time, the countdown was down to forty–five seconds.

"FORTY–FIVE SECONDS," whispered the MC through his microphone. The volunteers rocked back and forth on their heels, only occasionally glancing away from the lid to smile at their fellow volunteers and to the awaiting crowd, or to check the area around the tank. They were looking for the escape hatch. The man in the white suit and red tie was blank–faced and stared more into the silent audience than he did in the direction of Underwater Jack.

As the clock ticked down—30...25...20 seconds—the tension in the audience began to grow palatable. People glanced at each other, smiled, and chewed the little bits of ice from their

MINUS 55

complementary water glasses.

"IT WON'T BE LONG NOW, FOLKS," MC said.

The clock hit ten and the flash of cameras started. As the time ticked down to five and then zero, the flash grew more intense. Sarah could feel the blue pulsing lights behind her—from the people in the cheap seats, as her father had called them. As the time descended into the negatives, the audience started fidgeting about in its seat and chattering at itself.

"ANY SECOND...ANY SECOND," said MC and then he glanced
over his shoulder at Buddy. Buddy was now staring at the steel lid—back and forth between steel lid and MC, crowd and steel lid, steel lid and stagehands.

Minus thirty-five. Sarah let out her breath with a big puff, knowing that she had hedged more than just a bit on her breath holding.

Minus forty-five. People were now taking pictures in bunches—every five seconds, every time the MC raised his hands and said things like "A FEW MORE SECONDS," and "ANY MOMENT NOW." The people on the stage began to move around—especially the man in the white suit—and those cameras kept flashing, flashing.

Minus fifty-five. The MC took a quick glance at Buddy and then started making wild motions with his hands—to the stagehands and others off the stage. There was a lot of rushing around, panic, although it seemed to Sarah to be happening as if she'd just stood up too fast.

She saw the white-suited man leave the platform, down the stairs on the back and quickly to the front of the screen. He was motioning more wildly than the MC, waving more and more people onto the stage. There was a lot of yelling, screaming, but Sarah couldn't make anything out of it. The audience was in a constant hum. Some of it was standing, some of it was still sitting, and much was continuing the flash of cameras, pumping away with those cameras.

There were hospital people, white–dressed, rushing onto the stage next to Buddy, and more stagehands were appearing. One of the hands onstage was on his knees above the tank and yelling at his counterpart. The counterpart was screaming to Buddy's side of the stage.

The people with Buddy parted, the stagehands and the paramedics, and a strong man with a sledgehammer came between them, up to the tank.

Buddy shoved the screen aside, revealing Jack in the brightly lit water of the stage. He was floating in the chamber, naked and motionless, one chain still connected to his neck. He looked relaxed, as if he was just floating there and thinking the whole thing over.

The sledgehammer man reared back his hammer and people backed away from him. After a pause, the strong man took aim at the center of the tank and struck true. The tank exploded with water and Jack's body dropped and flowed with it, lifeless, into the broken glass...

"Figments, Inc."

Two men in a Buick. New Year's Eve.

"This whole thing seems ridiculous," said Lyle Gardetto, reclining in the passenger's seat, allowing dead cigarette ashes to fall onto the front of his suit. He was reading over an official paper titled "Exercise Premise." It had been stapled to another, titled "Subjects List," but that sheet was now in the glove compartment on top of a box of shells. "We're not really gonna use this, are we?"

"That's the exercise, Lyle," replied Armand Locke, the driver and Lyle's partner. "It's what we're out here to do. Until we get the signal, that's it."

"It just seems a waste of time to bullshit around with people when we could just be waitin' for our signal. That's all I'm saying," Lyle said. He read over the paper some more, aided by the street lamps Armand was doing his best to avoid. He shook his head and took in some smoke, laughed. "This thing reads like a some goddamned movie script."

Armand didn't respond although he could feel that Lyle wanted him to. He'd been listening to the same story for weeks and didn't care to try to explain the importance of a diligently followed exercise to his partner, as it had been a failed undertaking in the past. He just couldn't wait to get out of the car and finally take a good breath, really breath one in all the way. He'd been dodging cigarette smoke for more than an hour, leaning toward his open window, and listening to too much of Lyle's pick of the radio. The atmosphere, coupled with the driving, was beginning to make him sick with motion. He was ready for the business to begin. He was ready to open up shop.

ODOM

Agent Locke checked his watch and pulled the blue Buick up to a sidewalk after making the appropriate left–hand turn just down the street from the only house of consequence—a white one–story number that sat in the patchy, green grass of stereotypical suburbia. An odd place for Lyle and Armand's type of business, but they figured themselves adaptable. Armand rolled up his window and got out of the car, locked and shut his door and leaned against the side, next to the rearview mirror. He took one deep breath after another, each a combination of night air and the cigarette smoke that seemed to be hovering around him, woven into his suit and stuck to the bottoms of his shoes like a layer of the shit that collects on the floors of movie theaters. He looked around at the assembly line houses—every other one single–story jobs and the ones in between, double–deckers. A merger of architecture and bad taste.

It was nearly midnight, Thursday, and teetering between two years. It was a lack of celebration, however, that filled the neighborhood. It was dead, like there was no one else onstage— –no one else around. The only sounds available, short of the muffled radio through the window, were that of late–night songbirds and a sparse hiss of a traffic stream on a highway.

"Hey!" said Lyle from inside the car, still filling the interior with smoke. He seemed to refuse to roll his window down, although Armand had never heard anyone ask him to do any different. "Get back in. Let's go over this shit again."

Armand tried his door, but remembered locking it and so rapped his knuckles on the window. Lyle sat for awhile, listening to the radio and sucking on his cigarette. After a few seconds, he reached over and unlocked the door. Armand caught a last good breath and sat back down in the driver's seat.

"What do you want to go over?"
"Whatever. You've got ideas?"

MINUS 55

"Yeah," Armand answered, and he thought about his ideas. "OK. You wanna take your gun or me to take mine?" he asked, rolling down his window.

Lyle turned off the stereo. "What time is it?" he asked.

"Whaddaya mean," Armand said and he glanced at his watch. "It's 11:59. What difference does it make?"

Lyle wound the hands on his watch to the 11:50's. "Fifty-*nine*, you say?"

"Fifty-nine." Armand waved the hanging smoke out of his face and grimaced. "What about it?" he said. "You the gun or me the gun?"

"Why not both of us?"

"Because of this being an exercise and that's how we did it the first time, I just figured we ought to try something a little different this time."

Lyle took a drag off his cigarette and thought about his gun. "And how do you suggest we handle things this time?"

Armand looked back to Lyle and checked on how much cigarette he had left. "I'll do the talking and one of us takes a gun, just in case. That way I figure we can good cop, bad cop this guy if we need to."

Lyle nodded. "OK, I'm the gun," he said.

"Fine." Armand took his gun from inside his coat pocket and handed it to Lyle, who put it into the glove compartment on top of the sheet of paper titled "Subjects List." Armand checked his watch and yawned and stretched his arms back behind his head, behind the headrest.

"So what happened earlier, anyway?" Armand asked, again yawning and wiping at the corners of his eyes.

Lyle shrugged. "I don't know. I wasn't really getting anywhere with the guy, you know. I mean, you were in there, you saw that I wasn't getting through to the guy, right? I didn't want

ODOM

to waste all that time fuckin' around with 'im is all."
Armand nodded.
"He wasn't our man, anyhow, was he?"
Again, Armand nodded. "No," he said. "I don't believe he was."
"So what all do we know about this guy here, this next guy?" Lyle asked as he pointed down the street to the man's house. He had some more of the cigarette.
"He should be a better listener than the first guy, I think, all things considered," Armand said. "Still don't think he's gonna be our guy, though." He turned his head toward his open window and looked out into the neighborhood night. "He's a bookkeeper, an accountant, or was. Did some money laundering, that kind of thing. Got a little out of his league, I think. Made a couple big mistakes, got a little funny with the money so to speak. The guy's lucky he's still alive. Should be a good listener."
"Sounds alright to me."
"Yeah, I've got a better feeling about this guy than I did the first one. Still don't think he's our guy, though."
Lyle took in the last of his cigarette down to the filter and flicked the smoking butt past Armand's nose and out his open window. "What time is it?"
Armand took another long look at his wristwatch, took a deep breath and held on to it. "It's that time, I guess." Then he exhaled.
"You have your shitty script memorized?"
Armand nodded and laughed wearily. "Yeah. You ready?"
"Yeah, I'm ready."
They locked up the car, straightened their ties and walked their way toward the only important, one–story house on the block.

# # #

Armand and Lyle approached the house of Subject #2 like

MINUS 55

they were supposed to be there—like they were selling important vacuum cleaners or trying to convert somebody to their way of religious thinking. They approached as if their man was waiting inside, although they guessed that that wasn't the truth. Their agency–issue wingtips clicked like metronomes for the midnight songbirds as they glided along the paved sidewalk. It was quiet—no background—and the occasional patches of dirt scattered form yard to yard reflected the moonlight.

"Go on up to the door," Lyle whispered as the two agents turned up the walk, toward the front of the house. "I'm gonna check out this front window."

Gardetto hopped off the small concrete landing in front of the front door and moved through the wet grass to the large, illuminated window that was to the right. He peered through, trying to find the right angle that would allow him to see past the curtains and the glare of the moon. He moved from one side to another, looked through the bottom next to the white–painted window pane and up towards the top, aided by the tip–toes of his expensive shoes. He could see parts of the furniture, the carpet, seemingly untouched by a sole, and he saw the legs of a wooden chair sticking out of the middle of the carpet like shaved tree trunks. All bathed in lamplight.

As Gardetto squinted and adjusted, Armand looked around and waited for a signal to go ahead and knock on the door. "I'm gonna go ahead and knock," he said.

Lyle held up his hand. "Shh. Hold on," he said. He was still working every angle, both on his toes and almost kneeling. "I can hardly see a goddamned thing."

Armand looked around the silent neighborhood. "We're startin' to look a little fishy out here."

Lyle turned toward Armand with his head down and his hands on his hips. "Can't see anything," he said. Then he turned

ODOM

and started across the yard, whispering loudly over his shoulder to Agent Locke. "I'm gonna go around to the back. I'll let you in once I get inside."
    Armand started a question, but Lyle quickly disappeared around the corner of the house. He found his way through the gate of the chain link fence and into the backyard where the neighboring yards were surrounded, all of them, by tall, wooden fences, leaving no unwanted eyes on his action. He got to the back patio and carefully checked and slid the unlocked porch door aside, stepped very deliberately into the hallway. Everything was quiet except for the tick–tock of a wall clock somewhere in another part of the small house. It was loud like a tongue clicking off the roof of a mouth. The carpet was white and soft under his feet, and absorbed the squeak of his shoes like a light layer of snow. As he pulled his gun from his shoulder holster and made his way, in a crouch, down the hallway, he considered the possibility that some goons who were former associates of Mr. Rooney's had already been there or were there still. Maybe Subject *#2* had already been removed from the exercise.
    When he reached the first position he wanted to take, Gardetto stopped and pressed his back against the hallway wall. It was cool through the back of his shirt. He had come to the intersection where he could see the kitchen and the front door of the house, which opened into the living room he had previously been attempting to peer into. He prepared himself for what might be in that living room. He got himself ready to start shootin' at whatever moved, whatever seemed a threat. He took in a deep breath, slowly and silently, and let it out the same.
    After readying himself for every scenario he could imagine, Gardetto started the slow pivot into position—into the best strategic angle for a look at the living room—and he peered in.
    Atop the chair with the tree trunk legs stood Subject #2,

Chester Rooney, erstwhile bookkeeper of illegitimacy—a poorly fashioned noose hanging limply around his neck. The other end of the cord was knotted to a hook embedded in the ceiling. His head was down, eyes looking into the carpet, and he was wearing a Happy New Year hat.

As Lyle made his entrance into the living room, gun raised in potential self–defense, he said a quick "Hey," and Rooney turned and slipped on his chair. The line tugged hard on the ceiling hook as Rooney's black–socked feet slipped over the edge of the polished seat. The noose tightened for a moment around Rooney's neck and his face shot purple, but it didn't hold. It all gave way, sending Rooney, the hook, the noose, the Happy New Year hat, and a large chunk of white ceiling down hard to the floor.

"Jesus Chr*ist*," Gardetto yelled, with more an inflection of disappointment than surprise. He couldn't hide his laughter as he stabbed his gun toward its holster several times before finally landing it.

Armand, who had come in through the unlocked *front* door upon hearing the commotion, stood with his mouth agape and then quietly turned and shut the door. He wondered about all the noise, all the mess—and why Lyle was laughing.

As for Chester Rooney—he left his forehead buried in the carpet, not facing his house guests, who he assumed were there to murder him in a most unpleasant way, until Lyle pulled him to his feet by the starched collar of his white, well–pressed shirt.

Lyle turned to his partner and laughed. "Jesus Christ, man, I wish you wouldn't a missed that."

# # #

Armand sat, legs crossed left over right, on the chair that, in the report, the agents would refer to as the "suicide chair,"

ODOM

facing Chester Rooney and the coffee table. Rooney sat on the couch and Agent Locke's briefcase, sitting open toward its handler, was on the coffee table. Lyle paced the hallway, "Checking out the place for Mafioso," as they told Rooney, but it was actually because he couldn't keep his face straight after witnessing Rooney's failed suicide and seemed to uncontrollably ask Rooney "What the hell were you thinking with that hook?" Agent Locke was now in control, the master of ceremonies, as all of this conversation business was more his department.

Rooney was obviously shaken by all that was happening to him. He was frail, ill–looking. He kept closing his eyes and shaking his head, running his fingers through his thinning, gray hair and massaging the back of his neck. He had a twitch in his left eye that looked as if someone was pulling at it from off–stage.

Armand looked over a long sheet of agency–issue computer paper—lots of statistics and personal information on the subject of SUBJECT #2: CHESTER A. ROONEY. Every once in awhile the agent would punch the keys on the small computer inside his briefcase. Occasionally, a smaller sheet of paper was shot out of the printer on the side. Back and forth he went from computer to computer sheet, never once looking at Rooney—putting on the show.

Rooney was beginning to feel more and more nervous as the shock of his situation wore steadily off. The rational side was creeping back in on the emotions. He had been told previously, with a gun in his face, to "be quiet and let Agent Locke get some work done," and so he quietly twiddled his thumbs, looked about the dirtied room, and imagined what it would've been like if that ceiling hook would have held. What would all of that dying have felt like? He sat and thought about lots of things. He was anxious to find out who the hell these guys in his house were and why they hadn't put a bullet in him yet. The bookkeeper was sweating and that's exactly how Locke wanted to start this show. It was his addition to the plan, his creative input to the shitty movie script. He wanted Subject #2 to feel a sense a relief when he actually heard the story he had to offer him, wanted to build him up. In the end, he wanted #2 to feel happy and somewhat grateful. He wanted to successfully complete the exercise and get on with the business of finding their "Fight or Flight Man." All of this waiting and printing and reading was merely cosmetic, the set–up.

"Chester Arthur Rooney," Agent Locke read from the top of the longest sheet of paper. "Born 9–20–43, 9 pounds 3 ounces, to Tyler Lawrence Rooney and Mira Lee Rooney, at 11:39 in the a.m." He looked up from the sheet like a doctor or lawyer might and then, when no response was forthcoming, continued.

"You stopped growing at, roughly, the age of seventeen—five feet, eight inches—never broke a bone, never needed stitches, never had a venereal disease. You've had three cavities, none of which were properly cared for, and had three of four wisdom teeth removed." Again, he looked up. "Why didn't you have those teeth with the cavities taken care of?"

Rooney took his thumbnail out of his mouth and shakily answered, "I didn't want to go through all that."

Locke nodded and pouted compassionate lips. "That's understandable," he said and then picked up another sheet of the long paper and continued reading.

"You've rented 'Miracle on 34th Street' sixteen times? Man. Is that possible? Is that some kind of family thing, when the family comes over for the holidays or something?"

"Yeah."

"Hey, I know how that goes, man. I can understand that." And Locke sifted through more paper, only more briefly now.

ODOM

Finally, after impressively spitting out some more of Rooney's pointless information—vacations taken, favorite grocery items, lots of small financial transactions—Agent Locke organized all of the sheets and scraps of paper, many of them blank, into a pile and put them away in his briefcase. He uncrossed his legs and leaned forward, elbows onto his knees, hands hanging down between them.

"I bet you're wondering who the hell we are and what the hell we're doing in your house, interrupting your whole suicide attempt and everything," Locke said.

"I was...yeah," Rooney answered.

"Well, first of all, we're not with the mob. I can assure you that."

"What do you know about the mob?" Rooney asked and he leaned forward, began rocking back and forth.

"Well, I know you weren't hanging yourself in your living room because you knocked up a sixteen year old."

Rooney didn't have anything to say to that, and the two sat and stared at each other for a few seconds.

"You took a bit of mob money, am I correct?"

"Who the hell are you if you're not with the mob?"

"You could say we're federal agents."

"I'm not familiar. Be more specific."

"B.A.D." answered Locke, "F.I. division," and he reached into his inside coat pocket to retrieve his credentials. Rooney could see the empty shoulder holster with the coat pulled back. It was both a calming and sobering sight.

"What's the B.A.D.? What's that stand for? I've never heard of it."

"It stands for The Bureau of Astronomical Destruction. It's very hush–hush, top–secret, so don't expect to have heard of it." Locke handed his badge and paperwork, all neatly kept in an agency–issue, leather wallet, to Rooney. Rooney examined them for awhile, occasionally glancing up at Agent Locke.

"So that's how you know all of that...all of that personal stuff? You got it from my file?" said Rooney, his voice quivering like he'd been up for days *and* had fifteen cups of coffee..

Locke nodded, kept on nodding as Rooney was taking all of it in.

"Bureau of what, again?"

"Astronomical Destruction."

"B.A.D." Rooney shook his head.

"It's legit," Locke said, and he began with his story—the story in the exercise premise. "The Bureau is concerned with threats from sources outside the earth and its atmosphere on the lives of human beings, namely American human beings," Locke explained. "Over the past few decades, other countries have dissolved their programs that resembled ours, for economic reasons mostly. For several others who had the money to expend in that area, programs like the B.A.D. were deemed to be a waste of time and resources."

"This is some alien shit?"

"No, no, no. That's certainly not what this is all about. However, if that sort of thing ever cropped up, the Bureau would handle it, I suppose," Locke said. "But actually, my partner, whom I sincerely apologize for, and I are here to ask a sort of favor of you." Locke sat back against the chair and once again crossed his legs. "We believe we can help each other out. You help us and we help you."

"With the mob?"

"Yes."

"I'm listening."

Armand gathered the story in his head. He had it down—all the ins and outs, all the answers to all the questions. He was

ODOM

ready to weave a little business. "I need you to hear me out completely, Mr. Rooney. When you hear me tell you of the situation we're up against, and why we need you, you may be inclined to think I'm making all of this up. You may think I'm crazy. I assure you, on both accounts, I'm not."

Rooney nodded. He was ready for most anything.

"OK." Agent Locke exhaled a long breath through his nostrils and changed his crossed legs from left over right to right over left. His voice became stern and direct. "Chester, do you know what a martyr is?"

"What."

"A martyr is someone who makes great sacrifices for a cause or principle, someone who gives his life, his single life, for the whole of the group. Kinda like taking one for the team. You're familiar with that?"

" A utilitarian?"

Locke nodded, thinking, still playing with the storytelling options in his head. "Sure, a utilitarian," he said, and then he went forward with the story. "The world is in big, big trouble, Chester. And what the world needs, you see, is a martyr."

Agent Locke stood up and ran a hand through his hair. He walked over to the window and pulled back the curtain, allowing Rooney to look out into the world and the moonlight to come tumbling through the window, down from the heavens.

"You've heard about how the dinosaurs died, haven't your Mr. Rooney? Became extinct?"

"I think," Rooney answered. He was shaking his head, trying to go along. "The Big Bang?"

"Sure. The whole asteroid thing."

Rooney nodded.

"Well you see, Mr. Rooney, we as a race face a similar fate," Locke continued. He gazed out the window, out into the horizon. He got the feeling that maybe he was rushing things just a bit so he took some pause. He wanted to ease this one home, get Rooney going in his direction, pump him all up with patriotism, get a pen in his hand so he could sign the proper consent forms and get the show on the road. The pause allowed the moon to illuminate his face, making it glow and reflect brightly in the window. To Rooney, there were now two Agent Locke's—one looking off into the great beyond and the other staring directly at him. "As we speak, Chester, an asteroid nine and three quarters miles across is headed straight for us. The one that killed the dinosaurs, for comparison, was only six."

Armand paused again to let Rooney get the picture in his mind, the picture of dinosaurs running from fireballs and people running from slightly bigger fireballs, and then he continued. "It's these kinds of things that the Bureau keeps up on. You see, we've actually known about this particular asteroid for a very long time. With our equipment, which has always been many years ahead of our competition's I'm proud to say, we've been able to chart its progress whenever we had the opportunity." Agent Locke spoke assuredly, like he knew every word to be indisputable fact. "It was believed, based on our most recent calculations, that it was going to miss us by a considerable margin. But we picked it up again two weeks ago, ahead of schedule and off course."

Rooney sat quietly on the couch and let Agent Locke do his work. He was looking through the window and onto the moonlit street for cars that mob members might drive—Cadilacs…Oldsmobiles, back and forth under the street lights. As for Locke's story, he believed the agent to be perfectly sane, but allowed that he himself might be stark, raving mad.

"And what would all of this have to do with me?" Rooney asked.

"Let me continue," Armand said and walked back to his

ODOM

chair. The curtain stayed open, pulled back and hung on a brass holdback. "We never considered this asteroid, which we refer to around the office as 'The Super–Massive', a major threat because of the fact that it was figured to miss us and because we always relied on the fact that we could blow it up if necessary.

"I mean, just send a hydrogen bomb up there, strapped on the back of a computer guided rocket and BOOM!" Agent Locke made all the hand signals, from take–off to booming conclusion, selling every bit of it. "Everything would be taken care of, you know what I mean?"

"Sounds right."

"Ahh...but there was a problem," Locke said, both nodding and shaking his head. "One big problem. One problem big enough to completely prevent us from protecting the planet like we had always thought we could."

"And what was that?" Chester Rooney asked.

"The computers wouldn't do it."

Rooney shook his head. "I don't understand."

"Those guys' big brothers," Locke said, pointing to his briefcase. "They wouldn't guide a rocket into outer–space and then detonate a mega–bomb for anything—no matter what we did or told them to do. They refused to do it."

Rooney sat with a perplexed look on his face.

"I know," Locke agreed, shaking and nodding. "I couldn't believe it myself, at first. But then, once it was explained to me, it all made perfect sense. Are you familiar with neuronetics?"

"Not really. Maybe. It sounds familiar."

"Neuronetics is a type of computer technology that closely mimics the workings of a human brain. Essentially, neuronetics computers can make decisions. Of course the emotional capabilities of a neuro–computer are no where near human, but they can make basic, logical, yes and no decisions and are often designed, the newer ones anyhow, to ask themselves certain types of questions and then rationally answer them. They are rather impressive."

"So why the problems?"

"All of the launches went flawlessly, with no human meddling. But when it came time for the detonation of the mega–nuclear bomb, the neuro–computer simply wouldn't do it. It determined, rather selfishly I feel, that it was more of an asset to humans alive, or functioning, than non–existent."

Rooney chewed at his thumbnail.

"The United States government, your government, Chester, has been trying tirelessly to find another way to solve this problem by using our tremendous technology," Locke continued. "Remember me saying how the B.A.D. was well ahead of the rest of the field as far as technology goes?"

"Yeah. Economics and that?"

"Right, right," agreed Agent Locke. "You see, much of this swift technological advancement has happened during the past two or three years, for the most part. A great deal, anyhow. And we kept it to ourselves, under our hats, and we just kept plugging away at all of our questions, all of the mysteries we'd found, and they began falling one after the other. We were breaking new ground everywhere, but especially in computer technology."

"And that's where these neuro–computers came in?" asked Chester.

"Exactly," Agent Locke nodded. "Exactly. We gained so much new knowledge, made so many new discoveries, that we never had the time to perfect each and every technology. We were placing one discovery on top of another, always working on the newest most diligently. And when that new innovation led us to another, we stacked the old on top of the older as best we could and took off after our latest revelation."

"Sounds good."

"Yes, but it turns out that that kind of unbridled progress is dangerous," Locke said. "What we created was a sort of hole in the technology—a gap. With the neuro–computer, we had the power to pinpoint a moving target in outer space and hit it with a spacecraft, but we couldn't blow it up."

"The computers wouldn't do it."

"The computers wouldn't do it," Locke repeated. He smiled at Rooney because he was going along. His chest swelled and he kept on driving. "Technology has failed us, Chester, and what we have to have is a human, an American human, to set things right for the entire world."

Chester Rooney's blood was pumping. He looked at the big hole in his ceiling and the pieces of white plaster scattered about the floor. He looked out the window. He thought about the mob. He thought about America.

"What we need from you, Mr. Rooney, is to go for a little ride, a journey, and press the button that will save the entire human race and life on this planet as a whole."

Lyle had come back into the room and was in a silent crouch at his partner's side, fingers folded under his chin.

"Why me?" Rooney asked.

"We knew you needed some help. And we didn't want to waste what little time we had trying to talk cowards into doing a man's job," Agent Locke answered.

The room was silent as Chester Rooney thought it over. It was a hell of a lot to take in—astronomical destruction, martyrdom.

"It sure beats the hell outta hanging yourself in your living room, doesn't it Chester?" Agent Gardetto said as he waved his fingertips in front of his nose so he could smell the tobacco.

"You can protect me from the mob in the meantime?" asked Rooney.

"Absolutely."

Rooney looked back and forth between the agents and took a deep breath. "OK. I'll do it. Let's go."

# # #

Agent Locke had slipped off, he and his computer briefcase, to Rooney's bedroom, which had one of the two phones in the house, and began to feed all the pertinent information into all the pertinent places—bypassing "main information" and going directly into the stuff that's not supposed to exist. Rooney had signed all of the appropriate forms, answered everything just the way he should've, and in no less than ten minutes Locke and his computer had done everything from establishing Chester Rooney's rate of metabolism to getting him sized up with a crash test helmet—one with stars and stripes all over it.

In the meantime, while all off this gadget wizardry was taking place, Agent Gardetto had a moment alone with Subject #2.

"Shouldn't I be packing or something?" Rooney asked.

"Nah. Don't worry about all of that. We'll have you all taken care of in an hour or so—new skivvies, new T-shirts, new threads from top to bottom," Lyle said. The agent was still pacing, only now about the room instead of the hallway. "You mind if I have me a cigarette, Chester?"

"Go ahead."

And Lyle had a lit cigarette in his mouth by the time the answer was finished. "Can I ask you a serious question?" Gardetto said, staring up into the small hole in the ceiling, the smoke from his cigarette going in the same direction.

"Wouldn't you?" Rooney asked.

"Wouldn't I what?"

ODOM

"Have tried to kill yourself," Rooney said.

"No, but that's not exactly what I was going to ask you." Gardetto exhaled and then drew another long drag off his cigarette. "I was wondering, did *you* really want to off yourself? I mean, really?"

Rooney stared.

"I mean, you couldn't have imagined in a million years that that noose or that ceiling, either one, was going to hold you. Not all that weight. You go what—135, 145?" Another puff of smoke. "And that *hook* for chrissakes. It's a goddamn hangin' plants hooks, isn't it?" Lyle was laughing.

"Yeah, it's a plant hook," Rooney said, stammering over his words.

Agent Gardetto squatted to the floor and picked up the noose—an orange, heavy–duty extension cord. "And *this*," he continued. "Do you realize that this thing only would've strangled you to death if that fuckin' ceiling and that hook would've held. You could've been hangin' there thirty minutes before you finally died. The knot's all wrong on this thing," Gardetto said and he tugged at the cord from both ends. "Nothing's gonna slip on this thing, nothing's gonna slip. You should've set this thing up so it keeps on giving you some line, keeps givin' you line, and then it slaps you, BANG!, and it's a done deal. You sure as hell don't want to be spinnin' around up there for half the fuckin' day, do you?"

Rooney rubbed his eyes and worked his jaw back and forth like he'd just been struck upon it. "What're you trying to do here?"

"Who, me? Just me standing here or the two of us doing all of this business stuff?"

"I know all about the business stuff," Rooney explained. "I just want to know what it is you're trying to accomplish with this whole noose shtick."

Gardetto frowned. "Shtick? I'm not familiar with that one, Chester, but it sounds like a bunch of shit to me," Gardetto said behind a puff of smoke. "And as for the whole noose rou-*tine*, as I would have called it, I was just trying to start a little conversation is all."

# # #

Locke, Gardetto, and Rooney left the house via the side/garage door. It was decreed to Rooney that he would take his car, a compact little number, and follow the agents to a location outside of town—a place in the country—where they would get down to the business of saving the world. They didn't want him riding in the Buick until they were certain they weren't being followed.

As Rooney was further informed, once they got to the B.A.D. there would be a minimal amount of training and paperwork, maybe an interview with a "recorder," as Armand had called it, and then a precise outlay of what was going to happen, including several hours of flight simulation. A basket of bullshit through and through, woven from facts and lies.

"Follow closely, Chester," Agent Gardetto said. "We'll keep a close eye on you." And he and Agent Locke slid back into the Buick.

Rooney looked around his neighborhood for a moment, around at the trees and the little houses, and then he fumbled for his keys in his pants pocket.

"That wasn't so bad," said Armand, who had rolled down his window in anticipation of a cigarette.

"He ain't done nothing yet."

"What do you mean? All we have to do is get him to the countryside and he's as good as gold. He signed all the forms."

"He just doesn't seem like the right kind of guy, that's all. I'm not sure there's much they'll be able to do with him," Lyle

ODOM

said and he sank down into the passenger's seat, lighting a cigarette on the way down. He rolled over a bit onto his right shoulder and looked through his window, into the night sky. "I've got all kinds of bad feelings."

"It's cancer."

Lyle smiled and took in some smoke. Agent Locke was poised to start the car. His eyes were fixed upon Chester Rooney sitting in *his* car about fifty yards or so down the road to his left. He waited, tapped his fingers on the steering wheel, and Lyle smoked and looked out his window.

When Chester Rooney's car exploded and lurched into the air, Lyle moved nary a muscle and Armand could only watch in wonderment. The car sat blazing under the midnight sun, rippling the air with fumed heat and gasps of big, black smoke.

"Well," Agent Locke said, shaking his head, and exhaling a deep breath. "You'd better get that list out of the glove compartment."

"Yeah. And you should probably be steppin' on that fuckin' gas."

"Internal Combustion"

Noon, January 2. Jack was lying in bed with the heavy bedroom curtains pulled tight across the windows, completely blocking out the sun. He heard the front door to his apartment close and the locks click into place —the big deadbolt, the little deadbolt, and the doorknob. Buddy was gone. It was a two deadbolt neighborhood.

Jack was still on top of his sheets, content to be rolled onto his right side and drowsy, content to allow his torn and stitched body to begin healing. There were fifty–five stitches altogether, although no more than six were in any one place. Most were on the legs, a couple sets on his upper arm. All were on the left side.

He was quiet, a little smile creasing his lips. It had occurred to Jack that the evening before the hospital stay had been a complete and utter failure, but he didn't care. It hadn't been boring and that's all that really mattered. Those people would remember him.

He remembered being revived, just having had the water pumped from his lungs and replaced with another man's breath. He remembered how much his chest hurt and how all that blood mixed with hot water looked. But the whole thing was easy, really. The entire episode was over by the time he came around and the bloody water and shards of glass only added to the spectacle, only built the whole thing up. All of that would be remembered.

Jack pulled the big blanket up under his chin and tucked

ODOM

it down in under his feet at the other end. The old dial clock next to the bed hummed and buzzed and occasionally clicked, but Jack's eyelid's got heavy and he drifted, as he often did, in and out of sleep.

# # #

The whole apartment complex was unusually silent. Usually, there were crying kids and spousal spats a plenty, often violent ones, but now there was none of this. Jack's thoughts drifted back to the tank and into the warm water. All was going well when the shackles and chains were slipping off his body, over his wrists and ankles, one after the other, as they had always done. The waist chain was a little more time–consuming than Jack had anticipated, but it eventually fell around his feet and clanged at the bottom of the tank, reverberating and sending clusters of bubbles racing to the top of the water, past his head.

Usually, Jack would have been done at this point—no neck chain to worry about, only a heavy, steel lid to throw open and an adoring crowd's affection to consume. He'd been down no less than two minutes when he first considered the neck chain. Never before. He'd been still with contemplation, chains and shackles lying at his freed feet, which floated a bit—the few inches the neck chain would allow.

Why the neck chain?

Those people would remember the neck chain.

# # #

Fully awake again and back on the right side, none of the stitches had failed as Jack had rolled onto his left during the brief sleep. He opened his eyes for only a second to check for dangerous intruders that might be standing over him and then pulled the covers back up to his chin and slept again.

# # #

Big Sarah had been the "One" back when Jack still knew

what one was——the last of Jack's Queens—and she was comin' in on radar. Jack looked around, tried to catch a glimpse of her amongst the crowd, which had just settled its eyes on him. He couldn't remember what she looked like. He couldn't get her goddamn picture in his mind and he couldn't see her, but she was there. That was apparent. This was the dream about the woman.

Jack was on the platform again with the holes sinking into the bottoms of his feet. He was bound more completely in the dream version, incapable of moving a muscle, and his whole body itched, not just his nose. He looked around for Sarah. He could hear her voice against the background hum, but he couldn't make out any of her words. He strained his eyes dry, pulled them hard against the sides of the sockets, and he saw her behind a glare in the second row. She was red and pink. Through the lights Jack could barely make out her face, although he could readily see that she was in a big chair. Where the big chair came from, Jack couldn't fathom. Nobody else in the dream had big chairs. Her feet weren't even touching the floor.

He relaxed, having her there. It made it OK for him to let go of more of his vulgarity. It made him comfortable. The crowd noise and the energy of the event was still there—that hum—but it didn't have the same impact with her being there. It was her first show in some years and it made Jack feel young again.

The MC garbled some words, but Jack couldn't understand most of it. It sounded like pure feedback. "GAAARRSHJACKAUDIENCEBLAH!"

The crowd roared and the platform bounced, almost spilling Jack to the stage below. As his air was punched out of him, he strained in conjunction with the chains to keep everything in balance. As his face was disappearing into the water, he was still trying to get Sarah's face into his mind.

# # #

ODOM

The air conditioning unit shuttered, working, and the clock continued to noisily grind out the time. Jack woke up with the first, fresh blast of cold air. He liked to keep it rather cold when he slept, so he could use the big blanket. He didn't care for sheets—not on top of him anyway. He used an old sleeping bag, unzipped, with the slick side down to his body. It was some kind of comfortable sleeping bag—a red one. Jack had snipped off all its laces down at the end—the laces used for tying the bag up— and he'd popped off the zipper so it didn't jingle and jangle. The contrasting noise—the bass sounds of the air conditioner and the clock along with the treble-y clink of the sleeping bag zipper— could drive Jack crazy on the nights his aching body would cause him to twist and turn in an uncomfortable sleep. Consistent noise in the room was OK. But when you added another voice of noise, another flavor like jingles and jangles, then you had music—weird music that's hard to lose. And that's bad for sleeping.

Jack only slept in short spurts during the night and morning, anyway. He was in and out of working order along with the air-conditioner.

He pulled the unfurled bag up tight around his body, which was becoming sore. All of the stitched up gashes were showing up on pain read-outs in his brain. Each one throbbed up and down the laceration line. He could tell which ones were longer than the others and which ones were deeper. Or, at least he thought he could.

Although the pain wasn't too bothersome (he'd had his share of stitches) it was *there* now. And that, along with the appliance noise in the room, produced strange music with words— words with painful connotations. And that kept Jack awake for many minutes before he was finally able to shove the injured thoughts out of his mind, replacing them with another dream about the woman.

MINUS 55

# # #

Sarah had been 27 for almost a year when Jack met her. She was almost exactly seven years younger than he was, beautiful, with caramel skin and chocolate hair. She was working five nights a week at a classy strip bar in Las Vegas—classy because of the lack of neon lights and the presence of a food menu. Jack was in town catching a musician friend's act—an old friend from the old circuit. Both he and Jack had "made" it—at least so far as they didn't worry about where the next drink was coming from.

Jack was having a hook, a whiskey and Coke, and the music was loud although he was sitting in a corner away from the big speakers. His friend had turned in a couple hours earlier and Jack had decided to spend the rest of his night with stage girls. It was a slow night, a few guys here and there at the tables, most of them alone, with most of the action up near the stage where it belonged.

Jack loved these places. Not so much because of the tits and ass that bounced around on the stage, but because of the atmosphere. These places seemed completely foreign to every other place—another world overflowing with loud music, stiff ten dollar drinks, guilt, filth, naiveté, expertise...

It was late—about 3:30 a.m.—and Jack was plenty drunk, sustaining the feeling with several hours of light mixes and cigarettes. He was between work, but only by choice. More was out there, of course. There are always large groups of people around who want to see someone risk their lives for the sake of their entertainment. That's the beauty of the whole thing. That's job security. Flamboyant attempted suicide never goes out of style.

Jack could feel the big, thumping noise and the ambitious stares of the dancers, but he watched the other patrons mostly— a sometimes dangerous idea if eyes got locked. Locking eyes in titty–bars can lead to drunken words and shit–faced fist–fights.

ODOM

But regardless, Jack knew he could get himself out of most anything he got himself into, even at a titty–bar.

And so the usual parade of women didn't really appeal to him—manufactured breasts, lackluster performances, hiding timidity. The whole thing, when Jack really stopped and thought about it (which he rarely did), was pathetic on both sides of the table—the women and their showcases and the men who howled at their friends and dangled one dollar bills out of their slobbering mouths and half–opened zippers. Maybe that's why Jack looked around so much. Sometimes, pathetic sights made him feel better.

About 3:45, the pretty ladies walked through the crowd offering their specialized services, twenty dollars a pop for couch jigs and shower dances. The stage hounds were soon scattered around the perimeter of the joint—tens and twenties in hand, some handing over their cards of plastic. Jack was one of the only "gentlemen" left for the actual stage show. None of the dancers had even approached him about a private dance. This, he figured, was because they remembered him from the previous night.

The next performer was named Cherry. Only two guys were left in the man–pit for Cherry's portion of the show, two of the more drunken "gentlemen" in the club. The music was still loud, louder maybe, if that were possible, and the lights were still flashing. The whiskey kept flowing from Jack's glass as Cherry took the stage—began gliding her goods across the auction deck.

"You need a drink or somethin'?" asked an approaching waitress. She was new, or at least Jack hadn't seen her before.

"You gotta light?" Jack had spilled his drink on the pack of matches he'd had a previous waitress bring him.

Sarah sat down across from Jack and lit his cigarette with a match. Her hair hung down around her face, black, and was soft lookin'. Her skin was smooth, like brand new, and her eyes

MINUS 55

were clear and white with deep brown centers. She was small and slender, but inspired more animalistic thoughts than anything Jack had seen strutting about the stage. She was a real one. She made Jack feel like he wasn't drunk.

They sat for a few minutes and watched the stage show. When the top came off and the breasts flopped like breasts sometimes do, Jack started the conversation.

"You must think I'm pathetic or something, hey?" Jack asked, trying his best to straighten out the slurred words.

"How do you figure?"

"You just offered to bring me another drink when this one is still full." He held up his glass. "You're trying to poison me."

"I just did that because I like you," said Sarah, yelling over the raucous music. "I thought I was helping."

Jack nodded in the wake of his cigarette smoke. He leaned back and took a look at Cherry. Then he leaned back in. "I see. Well, then, how did you know you liked me?"

Sarah leaned in, her elbows on the table. "I saw you in here last night. I pick up on things."

"Huh?"

"I say I saw you in here last night and that I pick up on things," Sarah repeated.

Jack nodded and took a drink. "If I saw somebody in here two nights in a row, I think I'd have to lean toward hating them. The customers, I mean."

The first song of the individual–freestyle–porn–medley came to an end and there was some silence around. Sarah took the chance to laugh a bit and smile at Jack. Jack took the same. As the music started back up for round number two, Sarah continued the conversation.

"So, if you saw the same person...or customer...in here two nights in a row, you'd *hate* them?" Sarah shouted and laughed.

ODOM

Jack nodded and took a sip of his drink.

Sarah pointed to a guy at the edge of the stage, a guy that had nodded off onto his shoulder. "That guy's been in here three consecutive nights."

Jack studied the man for a few seconds and then shook his head. "Alright...so maybe I can't hate *him*. I'm pretty sure he's the only guy in here who's had more to drink than I have."

"So there goes your theory," Sarah said.

"Yeah. I guess I should say that I know pathetic when I see it. I guess I pick up on things too," Jack said. Then he pointed to a drunken business jacket stumbling quickly toward the door. "See that? That's pathetic."

Sarah agreed. "Never seen him in here before."

Jack shrugged his shoulders and pouted his lips. Then he and Sarah watched the man as he made his way to the door. In one of the many mirrors, Jack could see that the man's zipper was down and his white shirt was pulled a little through the opening. He was a pathetic piece of shit.

The conversation halted for a moment as both Jack and Sarah gave some polite attention to Miss Cherry for the remainder of the second and final song of the set. Guys were still getting dry-humped around the mirrored perimeter of the club. It all seemed surreal to Jack for a few seconds, but the feeling was fleeting and did not return.

In front of Sarah sat a round tray, three glasses sitting upon it. The top of the tray was wet and the ice inside the glasses was melting and forming droplets around the outside, heated by the flashing sex lights. Jack wondered if this girl, whose name he had not yet discovered, had work to do. He wondered if he might potentially be causing her some trouble with her sitting at his table and all.

Actually, he hoped this was the case. If there was a potential conflict presented by her sitting and talking to him instead of serving drinks and producing cash for the club, that meant she *must* like him. She was interested, no question. The only other scenario Jack could picture was that Sarah was somehow a stripper who had come to his table only to seduce him into stuffing money into her pants, or lack thereof, at a later date. Maybe she danced some nights and waited tables others. Maybe that's why he hadn't noticed her the previous night. She had been performing in a more private transaction somewhere apart from the main action.

But she never did take the stage or ask Jack to stuff her with money. In fact, after she and Jack left that night, she never went back into that place.

# # #

There were a series of ringing bells buried in the strip music and Jack flipped over into a dream about a bacon cheeseburger and a man with a deadly, red squirt pistol. No shit. When he woke up, the man and the pistol were gone and unremembered.

# # #

Awake again. Jack was flat on his back and the air conditioner was going at it like it wanted to cool the world. It sounded the way it did after it had been on for awhile—a little more dedicated than at the beginning of a cycle—humming grooves in the air. Jack snapped his eyes open and closed, trying to wipe off the cobwebs. It was 2:30 according to the clock, so it was actually 2:40, 2:45. It was a pretty good nap. Especially with all the patchwork. He yawned and twisted his neck around to pop it, then he pulled the covers up to his neck and slowly bunched himself together.

He laid there staring at the white, speckled ceiling. He was fairly well–rested, but even so, he stayed in bed and rolled over onto his right side to protect the stitches. The cool, slick surface of the sleeping bag felt good on his torn skin. It made him feel better all over. He had a piss–boner but he just laid there for a moment and tried not to worry about it too much. Then he started to worry.

After gathering enough energy, Jack kicked the sleeping bag down to the end of the bed with a few thrusts from his right leg and he stretched his body out away from center as far as he could. He forced his eyes to stay open and soak up what little light there was in his bedroom. He wanted to wake up and push all the fantasies out of his mind. He felt like being productive, not just lying in bed bullshitting with himself about women and work. Productive, which to Jack meant mulling around the apartment finding things to do—things to eat up his day, things to accompany his whiskey consumption. Some days he took walks around the neighborhood to catch a sunset, to smell the garbage and refuse building up in the corners, to buy a book or paper to read in the absence of a working television. But most of his day was spent inside the apartment complex.

There was a big light in the hallway, just outside his front door. Sometimes, Jack would read the paper and have his first drink of the day sitting under the light with his back to the door. He could hear everything from there if anything was going on. But he didn't usually stay there long, usually not past the main section of the paper and then he would retreat to the living room or kitchen to think or read or maybe even both.

When he was working, Jack was traveling and living in one hotel after another and he generally kept the reclusive lifestyle. However, he did get out to train some and eat at the restaurants and drink at the bars. Sometimes he felt like a big shot when he was far from home, in a town or city where he was performing. He felt like a celebrity and sometimes felt like getting out and enjoying the good feeling.

Jack's feet swung off the side of the bed and hit the stiffened, short, shaggy carpet. He scratched the bottoms, pressed them into the floor and rubbed them back and forth until they were warmed up, feeling good and ready to carry him through the day.

It was tough getting around at first as Jack tried to reckon the truth of his stitches. After awhile it was apparent that they would hold and they stretched to a point of reasonable comfort.

Thrown over a big chair in the corner of the room, a few feet from the front corner of the bed, were a pair of red sweatpants. Jack slid them on slowly over his ankles and legs, keeping them from catching on the stitches. They were loose and baggy, thin and comfortable. When they were tied, they hung around Jack's hips just below his belly. Just above the loose elastic there was a line of five stitches in Jack's side.

He considered throwing on a T-shirt that was bunched up in the corner, but was comfortable enough with just the sweats. He ran his fingers back through his hair, pulled it all back, and took a few deep breaths through his nose. Then he was off to the kitchen, by way of the bathroom to take care of that piss, for the first drink of the day.

# # #

The coffee dripped behind Jack, over on the counter, as he stood over the front page of the newspaper that was spread out in front of him on the kitchen table. There was a coffee mug sitting next to the paper, already a quarter filled with whiskey. On the other side was an ashtray with a burning cigarette pressed down between two of the tongs.

Jack read the paper quickly, much more so than he once had. He felt bad that he had digressed into the kind of person who only read the first paragraph of a story or maybe just the

ODOM

headline. There were still days that he sat and read every word, but they were as rare as the days when he took a really good shower—probably not often enough. And then there were the times when the paper never showed up on the doorstep at all. Jack didn't know whether it was due to a shitty paper boy or a kleptomaniacal neighbor, but he was sure that the inconsistent delivery had screwed with his reading habits.

The coffee finished its cycle and sighed with steam and Jack pulled the pot out from under the dripper. He poured the coffee into the mug, into the whiskey in the bottom, and he took a little sip from the rim. It was hot, steaming from the center, and scalded the lips. He put the mug back next to the paper and continued with the third page, grabbed his cigarette and took a drag, then wondered why there were no stories about him in the pages spread out across his kitchen table.

"And it happened so close to home," Jack thought, "such proximity. Right fuckin' here…nothing about it in the paper two days later. No follow up story, no fuckin' pictures, no columnist. Nothing."

He finished the main section of the paper and quickly shuffled through the rest of the rag, slowing only for the sports section and to sip coffee. He let the cigarette burn down to the filter.

#

The living room was dark and brown–looking. Jack sat on the sunken couch, shaped by and showing the wear of many households, and watched the blank screen of his TV. It hadn't worked for months, only sat collecting dust on its cold, black surface. Jack could see himself and his half of the room in the reflection.

On the coffee table, next to where Jack sat his mug and cigarettes, was a bottle of pills, painkillers, that he had gotten while at the hospital. The label read "use every four hours as needed." He popped the white cap off the brown stem and popped two of the pills into his mouth. The coffee and whiskey mixture had cooled enough to allow him to wash the painkillers thoroughly down his throat.

Jack breathed deeply through his mouth to get rid of the lump in his chest left by the swallowing of the pills. Then he sat still and thought about what was going on inside of him. The pain, what there was of it, was pulsating from visible sources—gashes and slits up and down his left side. The medicine was working from the stomach, gaining access to the bloodstream and eventually the brain where it would block the pain receptors up there, inhibiting.

Or would the medicine stimulate the pain–reducing receptors, exciting them? Jack wasn't sure. It was just another thing he didn't know enough about or understand, so he decided it was all in his head and that placebo and whiskey was the only truth. Whiskey *tastes* like it's having its way with you.

Jack lit up another cigarette and smoke blew from his lips in a beam of grey. Then he put the cigarette in the ashtray, between two prongs.

In the TV screen, he spied. He watched himself move with the cigarette and the mug. He did things twice or several times, all different ways to see which he liked best—pulled the cigarette out of the ashtray and took a puff, held the ashtray in his left hand, crossed and uncrossed his legs. He practiced his double and triple takes.

When he finished his drink, Jack put the cigarette out and looked around at the other objects in the living room. In the corner, to the back of the TV stand, sat propped an acoustic guitar. He had received it as a Christmas gift from Buddy two years previously, but he never learned how to play. There were a lot of

ODOM

rugs and quilts and blankets, too, on the floors and chairs. They gave the room its comfort. Most of that stuff had belonged to Sarah. Jack had never managed to give them back to her.

He went back to the kitchen to fix another drink and to get himself out of the living room.

# # #

Jack sat in the kitchen, playing with his Abraham Lincoln cigarette lighter and drinking his new mug of hot coffee and whiskey. He sipped at it slowly, measuring the heat on his lips, looking around the room through the steam. There wasn't much to the kitchen. It could have belonged to an 80–year old widow, a serial killer, or a bad father with bad children and a pitiful wife. It was standard. Jack liked it a lot in the kitchen. It was a nice place to relax—no bothersome stimulation. There had once been a picture of Sarah that hung taped to the refrigerator, but it had become unstuck and fell between the fridge and the stove. Jack had tried to fish it out but it was really back in there, behind some muck, and the tape seemed to rededicate itself to sticking to things. It wasn't budging.

Jack took a few deep breaths and rubbed his hand over his hair. He pulled his hair back through his fingers as he inhaled. And for at least seven minutes, he managed to keep his mind on only the kitchen, his coffee, his cigarettes, and the lost picture of Sarah. He even tried to fish it out again, although he came up a failure.

In no less than eight minutes, however, Jack began to think back to the neck chain. The light above the kitchen was turned on by a chain and so Jack blamed it for putting the thought of the neck piece, which wasn't even a chain in the same respect, back into his mind.

Regardless, Jack picked up his possessions—the cigarettes the mug, the ashtray, Abe Lincoln—and started looking for where

MINUS 55

Buddy had put those escape chains.

# # #

Jack stood before the hall closet, next to the back entrance to the kitchen, with his three items in hand. The closet was open. He didn't see any sign of the performance chains and so he put the cigarettes in his pocket, took a good sip of the coffee and closed the closet door, kicking the bottom and forcing it over the carpet that raised up in front. The chains weren't in his bedroom and they weren't in the bathroom—hadn't seen them in the living room either—so Jack figured they must be in the spare bedroom.

The spare room was down the hall from the closet and bathroom, around the corner from Jack's room, and there was rarely any cause for him to go in there. The doorknob was tight as he turned it with his ashtray hand. He took a sip of the coffee and pushed the door open, flicked on the light. There was no immediate sign of the bag that carried the chains, but there was a big chest sitting in the corner, next to a mattress which was lying on the floor.

Jack opened the chest and the bag of chains was there. He knelt down in front of it, not taking care about the stitches and sat the mug and ashtray on the open face of the trunk's top, which was held at nearly ninety degrees by a couple small chains.

Jack pulled the bag open. It was wet. He took out the neck manacle and the chain that attached to the front of it and then scooted on his ass across the floor and around the open box so he could lean back against the wall. He held the manacle in his hands. Water dripped from it, making spots of darker red spreading out in the fabric of his sweatpants and forming together with other spots. Jack rubbed the cold metal of the brace between his fingers. When he moved it around in his hands, more water fell from the hinges.

He closed his eyes and rested the back of his head against

ODOM

the wall—the first signs of the medicine kicking in. His head felt lighter. He reached over for the coffee and took a couple big gulps. Then he finished off the bottom with a grimace and an "Ahhh" as he tasted the coffee grounds and the bitterness of the whiskey.

When Jack had moved into the apartment, the extra bedroom had been used for storage of his and Sarah's stuff as well as a place for friends to stay. But it had become nearly empty—just the mattress, the chest, and the wooden dresser in an opposite corner. It had developed a strange feel now that there were no boxes of books or dishes or clothes lying around—no signs of life.

Jack stood up with the aid of the wall, still holding the neck brace in his right hand. Some water ran slowly down his stomach into the elastic of his sweatpants and he scratched at it. Then he picked up the ashtray and the cigarettes, left the mug where it was, and headed for the door.

The equilibrium shifted in Jack's head as he got to the center of the room and reshifted as his hand gripped the cold brass handle of the bedroom door. He shook it off and patted his belly with the manacle hand. He could hear his stomach growling.

# # #

An ash fell from his cigarette as Jack sat the ashtray on the toilet seat. He wished that he'd brought a freshly filled mug of coffee with him, but the mug was in the spare bedroom and the coffee and whiskey was in the kitchen. He was in the bathroom and the painkillers were steadily and thoroughly working their way through Jack's brain as he sat against the wall between the white sink and white toilet, staring at the bathtub. It was a freestanding, oval number, white with four little feet sticking out from under the corners. There was a lip all the way around the top edge and Jack had fastened a blue fixture onto the side next to the wall that held his shampoo and soap and washcloth. Everything was bone–dry. The washcloth was stiff with soap and the green soap had fossilized, dried–up, white bubbles and suds all over it.

Jack closed his eyes and rubbed at them. He took a long drag from his cigarette. He was thinking about the escape again— holding the manacle in his hand and leering at the tub.

It was strange to Jack, the feeling of failure, coming up short in the one area where he felt the most competent. He'd never botched an escape, at least not in decades. When he was much younger, a kid, he'd blown a few gigs by tipping his hand to his audience, but this was just in front of bar drunks and family. It's much more wrecking to fail in front of complete strangers. As Jack sat on the tile floor, his feet playing in the green rug between the tub and the toilet, anxiety rose up in his stomach like battery acid, up into the bottom of his throat. He felt directionless—like there was nothing pushing him from behind and there was no certainty in front of him. Stagnation.

The medicine was really starting to kick now and Jack put his head between his knees and drew deep breaths in through his mouth. He felt half asleep, half dreaming. He raised up onto his knees, in front of the bath, and winced as the stitches in his left knee tugged where they strained to bend with the body. He twisted the bath water on and put the stopper in the drain. Hot water drained out of the nozzle, but not very fast, so Jack put the cold water on a little, too. He was leaning over the tub, rubbing the bottom of it with his fingertips, rubbing them across the black–stained white and scraping little skids of dirt and scum off the bottom. Before long, Jack's hand was overcome with the lukewarm water. It felt good. It made him have to pee.

ODOM

"The New Scent"

Subject number five was just as dead as numbers one through four. She lay, chest to the floor, next to her living room couch—a blue one with pastel flowers all over it. There was a halo of blood growing into the carpet around her head, red instead of glowing gold like the ones in those old religious paintings they say lacked dimension. Lyle Gardetto was holding his weapon.

"So, whaddaya think?" Gardetto asked Agent Locke, but Locke had already turned away from the scene, somewhat disgusted by Lyle's apparent pride in his work, and headed back to the bedroom where he had his computer hooked to the woman's phone line. He had his own work to do.

First, Agent Locke created Miss Arnold's financial problems —overdrawn checking account, depleted savings, over-used credit, outstanding payments—one reason after another. All part of the exercise. Meaningless, but part of the exercise. With Candy's card, Locke sent the whole of the dead girl's savings to charity organizations—mostly to an abused women's shelter, one that probably serviced Armand's conscience more often that it did abused women. What little was left in the girl's checking account was transferred to the Bureau's coffers, all but nine dollars and seventy-three cents. The crumbs were left for subterfuge.

Next, he registered Miss Arnold the owner of the weapon that had killed her—the gun Gardetto was holding in the living room. He gave it a history—where it was purchased, how it was paid for, the training or lack thereof that she had acquired. He covered everything. The gun was her's.

Third was the suicide note—a short one scribbled in Candy Arnold's handwriting, a perfect sample right down to the signature. Agent Locke used his computer's printer and printed it out on some stationary he'd found in the kitchen next to the telephone and then he checked it against Miss Arnold's checkbook and some notes she had left on her refrigerator.

Everything was in order. Candy Arnold had killed herself because of financial problems and an unjust world. Silly reasons, but good enough. Armand sat the note on the bed and then closed his briefcase with his gloved hands. He sat for a few moments on the corner of the bed and stared into the plain, yellow wall. He tapped his fingers on the computer case and glanced at the note, looked at the desk and nightstand, looked at the yellow doors in front of the closet. He was trying not to think about the bloody girl in the next room, trying not to think about his partner standing over her with his big, inappropriate smile.

He'd known the girl was as good as dead when he walked into her apartment. He knew it was already in the cards long before he and Lyle ever arrived. She'd have walked in front of a bus or fallen down a sufficiently long elevator shaft in a few minutes anyway, he thought. This is how all the "Subjects" were chosen for the exercises. They were in the "ready to go" group, as Lyle was fond of calling it. But that wasn't much consolation for Armand. The exercises were still a hard thing for him to be a part of.

From the corner of the bed, Armand adjusted his tie, pulled the knot down a bit and undid the top button of his white shirt. He was tired. It had been a roller-coaster three days. From the explosion of Chester Rooney to the "suicide" of Candy Arnold, things had not gone well. The entire exercise had been an emo-

ODOM

tional bust and the agents were facing going home empty–handed. Locke grabbed his briefcase by the handle and pinched the corner of the suicide note—stood up with both of them. On his way out of the room, he stopped and sat them both down, the briefcase on the floor, the note on the briefcase, and returned to the bed where he gave a healthy tug to the yellow blanket and tossed the yellow pillows around the room like he was angry at them. He shuffled the sheets and pulled the mattress cover off, left it all in a yellow bunch. Then he returned to the living room.

"Got it?" asked Gardetto.

"Yeah, I got it," Locke answered. "You take care of the gun?"

"Yup. The fingerprints are on the gun."

"Why're you still holding it then?"

Lyle smiled. He was smoking a Virginia Slims 100, holding it with a hand wrapped in latex.

"Those her cigarettes?" asked Agent Locke.

His partner nodded.

"Good. Nice to see some thinking."

Locke put the suicide note on the coffee table so whoever found the girl would quickly find out why she was laying in a pool of her own blood. Then he looked for a moment at Agent Gardetto, who was still holding the gun in his gloved hand, holding it up beside his head.

"How 'bout putting that gun on the floor next to her left hand so we can get outta here," Locke said. "And stick her index finger through the hole...where the trigger is."

Gardetto walked around the coffee table and his partner and over to the girl, where he knelt beside her. Locke wasn't watching. Even though he knew he should be keeping an eye on the specifics, he wasn't fond of seeing all that blood and so kept his eyes on a painting of a landscape that hung crooked on the wall. In the corner of the canvas was written "L. Arnold." Probably a relative, Armand thought. Maybe a grandparent or parent. Maybe the person who would eventually find that suicide note.

"You done?" asked Armand.

"Yup."

"Finger in the hole?"

"Yup."

Gardetto stood up and straightened his tie.

"You did shoot her in the left side, didn't you?"

"What difference does it make?"

Agent Locke didn't answer.

"She's left handed, isn't she?"

"Let's get out of here."

Armand took one last look around the room. Everything was set up. The agents left quietly, locked the door behind them and returned to the car which was parked down the street a couple blocks and around a corner.

Lyle climbed in on his side and lit a cigarette. "Five down," he said.

Agent Locke rolled down his window and pulled the car away from the curb. The latex smell on his hands was almost as bad as the cigarette smoke.

# # #

The Buick bounced down the highway, twenty miles an hour over the posted limit. Lyle was now driving as he and Armand had switched seats at a gas station a few miles back. Agent Locke was actually enjoying the trip now. His window was down all the way and Lyle's was cracked open a little at the top, just the way Armand had left it. His ventilation plan was bearing fruit.

It was ten minutes before the next highway turn. The sun was out and the sky was blue and wide open. It was a fine day

ODOM

and the light breeze and the upcoming countryside started to push the bloody girl out of Armand's mind.

Lyle puffed away on his cigarette, the smoke trailing up to the opening at the top of his window and getting sucked out into the nice day. He had ceded control of the radio to Armand and the dial sat on an oldies station—nice old tunes. Candy Arnold had been off Lyle's mind for miles now. He'd left her at the gas station.

There wasn't much to talk about now that they had lost all of their possible subjects. Their work was complete for the time being and their relationship beyond the professional was pretty limited. They drove on, Lyle smoking and Armand enjoying the smoke rolling out into the nice day. They drove, listening only to the radio and the wind, until Lyle took an unanticipated turn.

"Where're we going?" Armand asked.

"Let's go see Jon."

Armand shrugged. No objection.

# # #

Jon Strong had been a B.A.D. agent before he went crazy. Both Lyle and Armand had worked with him at the Bureau, Armand prior to Lyle and he had hated him more due to the more comprehensive exposure. Strong was the kind of guy that lords his seniority over you, makes you do all the cleanin' up. He went crazy one day when he went out on his own—just came back crazy, saying crazy things. The clincher, of course, was that he didn't think there was anything wrong with how he was acting or what he was saying, thought his every utterance was misunderstood wisdom.

As far as the quality of his work before he was sent away ill, Jon Strong was the best at getting things done. He was a great motivator of strangers—good at convincing them to pull themselves up by their own bootstraps. And so, for this reason of quality, occasionally, Lyle and Armand, as well as other Bureau members, would go out to see Jon in the hospital, see what he had to say. They would go for that and to watch him act crazy and think crazy, say crazy things. For some, Jon Strong was a true marriage of business and pleasure.

# # #

The back way into the hospital wasn't paved—gravel—and just like the Bureaumen always requested, Jon Strong was standing out back waiting for them. An orderly was standing next to him.

"Pull up over there," Agent Locke said, motioning to a spot designated by two spray–painted lines, next to the back walkway. Gardetto eased the car in.

Armand was out immediately, shutting his door tight behind him, and walking over to the two men standing at the back of the hospital. Gardetto finished his cigarette, crackled it all the way down to the filter, and then put it out real good in the ashtray. It was hot in the car now. All of the windows were up, and the shade from the building and the nearby tree missed the car completely, giving it up to the sun. Lyle sat for a moment until he could feel the sweat coming. Then he, too, got out of the car.

Locke was already talking and shaking hands, although Jon Strong was obviously not all there. He shook hands with a limp left and then wiped it off on his white pants and shirt. His right arm was completely paralyzed, although only by his own mind. There was no physiological reason for it, they said. He was crazy.

"I thought he was supposed to be unmedicated," Gardetto said.

Locke answered him. "He should be coming out of it soon. They skipped his last two..." Locke searched for the word

ODOM

and snapped his fingers.

"Doses," said the orderly.

"Doses." And then Armand made the introductions. "This is Agent Gardetto. Agent Gardetto, this is Manny. Manny doesn't know anything."

"Not one thing," said Manny.

"Good. It's good to meet you, Manny," said Lyle.

Gardetto and Manny shook hands. Lyle stood there looking over Jon Strong for a few seconds. Strong was just standing there, looking around and breathing. He was damn–near catatonic. Lyle waved his fingers in front of his face.

"Does he still smoke?" he said.

"He doesn't do much of anything," answered Manny.

There they were, three men looking at the one—the one looking at nothing in particular. Perhaps the car, or the gravel or the birds in the grass. Probably nothing.

"Does he ever say anything?" asked Locke.

"Only when the doctors want him to."

"And how do they swing that?"

"They just take him off his medication."

They were all still looking.

"So he'll talk to us a little later?" asked Locke.

"He should snap out of it any time. Then he'll start to talk," answered the orderly. "You probably won't get much out of him, though. Nothing but the supernatural gibberish."

"I thought you didn't know anything," said Gardetto.

"Nothing about what you guys are doing here. Nothing about that." Manny continued. "They're always shootin' questions at him after he comes off the stuff, though."

"About supernatural gibberish?" Lyle asked. He laughed.

"Yeah. So when he comes around he'll probably go right into the transmitter, paralyzed arm, supernatural shtick."

"Shtick?"

"Routine," said Manny.

"So, that's what we have to expect," Armand asked.

"Almost certainly."

The agents nodded their heads, still looking at Jon Strong who was looking at everything or nothing. It was cool under the shade tree and closer to the building.

"Well, Manny, you've been a lot of help for not knowing anything," said Agent Gardetto, shaking hands again. "We'll not have to kill you now." He laughed.

Manny laughed nervously, said "OK", then turned and walked back into the hospital.

Jon Strong wanted to follow him and turned to go, but Lyle got to him before he made the door and grabbed him by the arm. "What do you say, Jon. Let's you and me go for a little ride."

# # #

Jon was moaning in the back seat. "Out…Out…out…out…Out…"

The agents were expecting supernatural gibberish stories and considered the moaning to be evidence that they were coming. They had figured Jon wouldn't like the car, but they drove on for a couple of minutes to clear the sight of the hospital.

"Get out…Out…oUt…ouT…oUt…out…Out," Jon repeated over and over again in different pitches and cadences, like he was rehearsing for his big role, running scales.

Lyle pulled the car over next to a hilly area—a lot of bright, green grass in the sun. It looked as though this wasn't part of the hospital grounds. It was sectioned off with a long row of carefully placed trees—a natural fence. The line of green stretched on for a long way, back into a densely wooded area.

Locke got out of the car and hopped over a little ditch. It

ODOM

was dry, but he jumped it anyway. He walked up the first small hill and stopped at the top, stared out over the other small hills and the big one in the middle. It looked like a model for a golf-like game he'd once imagined where there is a race for the 18th hole—the center hole, the one up on top of the biggest hill. He'd let a handful of people in on the concept but many of them regarded it as just another shitty idea.

Locke headed toward the big hill in the middle of the rolling field—to give Lyle and Jon some time together, and to think about nothing for awhile.

# # #

Gardetto, still in the driver's seat, was smoking a cigarette and looking at Jon Strong in the mirror on the back of his sun-visor. Strong had stopped moaning once the car had stopped and Lyle knew, from his understanding of shattered, human essence, that Jon would most definitely feel safer in that car than he would in that wide open field.

Gardetto took in a good breath. "C'mon, Jon. Let's go for a walk."

Jon looked around in Agent Gardetto's direction. He seemed confused and lost—like he'd been hit over the head with something—but it was like he was almost there now.

"Jon."

Jon looked.

"Can you get out of the car, man?"

Jon took a deep breath and shuddered a bit when he exhaled. He reached across himself and grabbed for the door latch with his left hand. He took another breath—his face blank—and then he opened the door.

Both Jon and Lyle were out of the car now. Armand had moved on to the next hill, a little further out into the clearing—hole five or something, the front nine. The sun was still baring down, but there was a light breeze that seemed to be coming from the woods that cooled everything.

Back at the car, Jon was staying as close to as he could, touching it at the top with his left hand—his right, limp at his side. He was still looking around—above himself, behind himself, out into the trees, and at Armand, who was getting smaller to his right.

"You wanna walk with me a little?" Gardetto suggested. "Maybe over to that line of trees."

Jon looked over to the green line and nodded his head. Lyle took him by the elbow of his limp arm and began walking him slowly toward the trees. Jon slid his hand across the top of the car as they walked. He seemed like a very old man.

"OK?" Strong asked.

"Fine, Jon. Everything's fine. Like old times, you and me."

They were clear of the car although Jon kept his left hand out toward the side. They walked slowly. Locke reached the third hill.

"So how do you feel about talking to me?" Lyle asked.

"OK."

"Good. Just a little talk. Just like old times, you and me."

Gardetto always felt strange leading Jon Strong around by the arm. It made him feel uncomfortably powerful. Strong had become an old man of only forty-nine years. His grey, slicked back, greasy hair was gone, replaced by the hospital cut—buzzed all over, short to the scalp. And he was crazy.

Gardetto and Strong reached the line of trees and Jon reached out for one of them. He looked around the shade, looked at the broken sky though the tree branches. He looked back at the car and then to Lyle.

ODOM

"You get out much? You like to walk around this place?" Lyle asked.

Jon shrugged. "You know," he said, "a stranger in a strange land..." He inched closer to the tree and put his arm around the bark like it was his lady. He held on to her and looked about and around himself, above and behind.

Lyle looked around too—for Jon's sake, checking things out, making sure Jon noticed him.

"You alright, Jon? The coast is clear. No need to be nervous."

Strong held tight to the tree and continued his look around the area.

"Agent Locke and me aren't gonna let anything happen to you out here. You know that, don't you, Jon?"

"Yeah. It's alright. You guys are alright."

Lyle was nodding his head. He was proud of the way he was handling all of this. He wasn't usually the one to do all the talking, but he and Armand had decided on the way to the hospital that it would be good if he took care of this one.

Agent Locke was to another hill now—they were rolling toward the clump of trees to the West. He was walking toward the 18th hole, the one that leveled out on the top, the one that was nice and easy. He wanted to clear his mind, stand in the soft grass and allow the sun to have him for awhile.

"You want a cigarette?" asked Lyle who had a Marlboro between his lips and another in his hand, out toward Jon.

Jon stepped away from the tree, left his hand touching the bark. He looked back at his lady and she looked on past him.

"Marlboro?" Jon asked.

"Yep."

Jon reached out and grabbed it tentatively from Lyle's hand. Then he went back to the tree.

MINUS 55

Armand reached 18. The sun lit him and the ground was soft below his feet like carpet, like he knew it would be. He stood and looked around at the trees and through the trees in a line and out into another field, a much smoother one. Armand turned in a circle—saw the tree line, the big clump of greens, another line, the car, and then Lyle and Jon Strong. Their heads, anyway. He squinted to try and see if their lips were moving in conversation, but couldn't make out the details. He assumed, however, that things must be going fairly well because he could see both their heads. They weren't rolling around on the ground, Lyle wrestling Jon, who was of course crazy.

Jon smoked his cigarette and smiled some. He would laugh a short burst and shake his head when he inhaled the smoke. It seemed to bring him back a little.

"So things have changed a lot, huh Jon?" said Lyle, who was pulling out two more cigarettes. He put one between his lips and the other behind an ear.

"They say I'm crazy," answered Jon, nodding and rocking on his heels. He looked down at his cigarette, which had come to its conclusion.

"Just drop it down and step on it, man." Lyle pulled the other cigarette from behind his ear and lit it for Jon and then handed it to him.

"You think you're crazy, Jon?"

Jon paused and looked up to where the smoke was hanging. "A sane man in an insane world is an insane man."

A sane man in an insane world is an insane man. Lyle didn't know quite how to follow that. He kind of liked it, though. It was worth the gas that had been burned to bring he and Armand out there, worth the price of admission.

Armand stood on the biggest hill. It had just gotten a little cooler now that the wind was taking over the hills. The sun

ODOM

had gone in behind some clouds.

# # #

Armand reached Strong and Gardetto shortly after he could no longer see both of their heads—just the top of Lyle's. Jon Strong was sitting on the ground, mumbling incoherently and sobbing.

Locke asked what the hell was going on.

"I don't fuckin' know," Lyle answered, whispering through his teeth. "It was goin' fine for awhile. We were talking."

"Well, we'd better take him back," Agent Locke said.

"Yeah. Let's get him back in the fuckin' cage."

Armand said hello to Jon and Jon looked up at him. Lyle got him to his feet and Jon started wiping his eyes with the sleeves of his long, white shirt. His white pants were dirty from the ground, but neither agent dared wipe him off. He was fragile, like a little bastard kid in a grocery store.

"Let's get him back," Locke said. "You walk with him and I'll take the car back."

Armand started to walk off, but Lyle stopped him. "Why don't you walk him back."

"OK," Armand said. It was fruitless to argue.

Lyle turned and walked toward the car. He lit a cigarette and turned his head toward the sky, whispered to himself, "A sane man in an insane world is an insane man."

# # #

When Armand arrived with Jon Strong, Lyle was sitting in the lobby reading a newspaper. Armand held Jon by the elbow, the good one. They were both sweating a little.

"Where is everybody? Where's Manny?" Agent Locke asked Lyle.

Lyle pointed to behind the front desk, back where a set of doors were.

74

"Manny!"

Manny came out. He was eating an apple.

"I'm need to return this," Armand said and handed over control of Jon.

"Did you give him a pill?" asked Manny. Armand frowned. "Oh, yeah, you guys wouldn't have any of the pills, would you," Manny said and kind of laughed just for himself. Then he took the patient away. Jon didn't acknowledge either of his former partners as he passed through the swinging, double doors just between the front desk and the couch Lyle was sitting on.

Armand let out a sigh and plopped down in a comfy chair next to Lyle. Lyle was still reading the paper. His hands were busy, one holding up the paper and the other clicking at his lighter or tapping on his cigarette box.

"You almost done with that paper?" asked Armand. He was a little out of breath from the walk.

"In a little while."

"You don't need a cigarette or anything?"

Lyle looked up at him and then back to the paper. Then he rustled it all, plucked out the sports section and handed it to Armand. With the rest of the paper tucked under his arm, he went outside to smoke a cigarette.

Armand hated sports. He could stomach baseball, but it wasn't baseball season yet. So, he put the paper down on the table in front of him, on top of some magazines. He felt like he was waiting to get his teeth cleaned, caught himself hoping the hygienist was attractive

Manny came back through the double doors. "How was he?"

"He was very bad. I left him alone with Agent Gardetto for a few minutes so he could work him over real good."

ODOM

Manny smirked.

"And that's it for your questions."

"Where did Agent Gardetto go?"

Agent Locke shook his head and turned away, spread his arms out on the back of the couch.

"Sorry."

"He's out front havin' a cigarette."

Manny walked over to the small hallway leading to the front door. He looked down it and then looked back at Locke. Then he went toward the door.

Agent Gardetto was pacing back and forth and looking at and peering over the top of the bushes in front of the windows. Cigarette smoke trailed from his lips as he turned his head.

"Hey," said Manny, conversationally, pushing through the glass door. "What's goin' on?"

"Trying to decide if I should piss in these bushes."

"Did Jon talk to you?"

"We talked. Not about much, though."

"Well, wha–"

"Do yourself a favor, Manny," Gardetto said and he pointed his finger at him. "No more fucking questions."

Manny turned and walked back inside where he disappeared through the double doors without a word to Agent Locke.

# # #

"What the hell are we doing now?" asked Lyle, leaning forward from the couch with his elbows on his knees. Armand was sitting back on the comfy chair, his legs spread, his tie pulled down a little, loose around the neck.

"I don't know. You just wanna head back? I mean, as much as I hate to come all the way out and then go home with no kind a success."

Armand was silent. He looked about the room and at his

watch. He checked his watch with the clock on the wall. "Yeah. Let's just get outta here."

Lyle and Armand got up and stretched. Armand folded the newspaper, all but the sports section, and tucked it under his arm. "Did you say anything to Jon about what we were up to?" he said.

"Yeah, I mentioned it."

"And what did he say?"

"He said it was going to take a sledgehammer and a fine-toothed comb," Lyle answered and laughed. "He answered that way for about five different questions."

"Anything else?"

Lyle held his wristwatch up to his ear and listened for a second. "He said a couple other things. You know what time it is?"

Armand looked at his watch and at the clock on the wall. "About noon. You've got a damn watch on."

"*Exactly* noon?"

Armand looked at his watch again and the wall again. "Noon."

Lyle reset his watch to the proper time and again held it up to his ear for inspection. "Yeah, he kept on saying things like, 'A sane man in an insane world is an insane man.' That kind of stuff."

Armand nodded. "Yeah, I've heard that one before."

# # #

The car was hot inside and the windows came down, which pleased Armand. Lyle lit a cigarette and backed the car out of its parking place and back onto the drive. He was behind the wheel so Armand could read the paper.

"This is yesterday's paper."

"Yeah, that's all they had back there."

ODOM

"Well...I guess I haven't read yesterday's paper either."

Agent Locke started with the first story on the front page. He kicked back and read, enjoying the wind in his hair while keeping the paper tight and under control against the gusts. He trusted Lyle could find his way back to the hive. There was windy silence until Armand hit the third page.

"I think I got us one," he said. "I think this is it."

"Strange Assistants"

Agents Locke and Gardetto were at the dotted line—the edge of both the country and the city. On the left was green field after green field, separated by a creek or a line of trees, and as they drove on there were little white houses and ponds, even the occasional cow. To the right, however, were auto garages and insurance businesses—white concrete and glass structures—and even deeper to the right, a city that went from bigger and bigger to big. The city concrete was slowly gobbling up the country green.

They were still over three hours from the Bureau and the agents were trying to enjoy their time away, as well as the unusual weather they found themselves away in. Armand read the newspaper. Lyle drove and smoked.

"I think I got us one," Armand said, reaching the third page of the paper, and he pulled his briefcase from behind his seat and opened it up in his lap. He punched around on the keys and information popped up on the screen and then gave way to other bits. He eventually got to a map—one with city concrete gobbling up country green. He studied it for a moment and then punched in more information—information that he checked with the help of a little notepad which he had used to take notes from the newspaper. Lyle could feel him working, so he let him employ the quiet.

"Lyle, how 'bout taking a right at the next intersection," Armand said, not looking up from the screen. "We've got us an affirmative. We need to get into the city."

ODOM

Lyle turned on the turn signal, changed lanes, and flicked his cigarette out the window. He pulled the car up to the white line at the next red light and watched as a young mother crossed the street. She was pushing a baby carriage and her long, brown hair and loose dress were blowing backwards toward the countryside.

# # #

The Buick pulled up to the curb and Armand filled Agent Gardetto in on the specifics. He told Lyle that their new man was around the corner a block and a half and living in an upstairs apartment of one of the complexes. He told him that the guy was "perfect machinery for our modus operandi." He further informed Gardetto that he would be doing all the talking—told him to sit tight unless something happened that was clearly threatening. Armand told him he could handle this one.

It was ridiculously warm for the time of year, especially without the benefit of wind stirring through a moving car. It was stagnant—the kind of warmth that compels people to talk about the end of the world, the apocalypse, but Armand and Lyle didn't discuss the weather.

"And we know exactly where this guy is?" Agent Gardetto questioned.

"Yeah."

"We know he's *there*?"

"Well no, we don't know he's *there*." Armand answered. "We're just gonna have a little faith. Keep up some hope, man."

Armand got out of the car. After checking out the interior of the car and locking it up, Lyle got out, too. It was damn hot inside those agency suits with the occasional, hot wind blowing from somewhere unimaginable. It was the beginning of January. All the warmth should have left town already.

Gardetto followed Locke around the corner and toward a

MINUS 55

tall building. The streets were empty as midnight.

"Can we keep this one, Pa? Can we keep 'im?" Gardetto said, speaking like Hollywood's version of a southern child. "I don't wanna have to shoot another 'un." He was laughing and walking little zig–zags around his partner, sweating.

Locke nodded and frowned. "That's very nice. I like that a lot, in fact." And the agents disappeared through the swinging front doors of the apartment building.

# # #

"That one don't work," said a little boy, maybe seven or eight, to Lyle and Armand. They were standing in front of the elevator in the lobby of the apartment complex. It was very dimly lit and even hotter inside the building than it had been outside—like the people running the place had no sense of what was going on in the atmosphere around them. It was like they lived in that place all of the time, chained to the center of the building by an ankle, doomed to perpetually serve.

The interior of the lobby was dark red where it was painted and dark wood where it was not. There were a lot of lights around and they were on, but they were shrouded by tinted glass and heavy shades. There was a section in the corner where a fat, bare–chested man sat with his feet up on a long coffee table. He was reading a magazine and smoking a cigar. There was that smell in the air. It seemed like everything had been there for many years—like the agents were walking into an old oil painting.

The young boy disappeared around a corner, through a set of propped open double doors that led to the numbered rooms. Past the front desk and the office and past all the mailboxes, Armand and Lyle followed the boy to the next elevator. When they got there, the up arrow had already been pushed, glowing a muddy orange, and the agents could see the little guy skipping

ODOM

and bounding away until he was gone around another corner.
 The agents stood and watched the semi–circle dial above the elevator fall from sixteen to one without pause. The doors opened to a vacant compartment and they stepped inside.
 "What number?" Lyle asked.
 "Fifty–five."
 Lyle pushed the corresponding number twice and it glowed. He pushed it again as the car bounced into working action slowly, sounding like a carnival ride. It was dark in there, too.
 "There seems to be a motif going here," Armand said directing Lyle's attention to the burned out bulb above them. A second was working.
 "Yeah," Lyle said and he lit a cigarette.
 The agents stood and watched the numbers as they were illuminated and then extinguished, passing the light to the next number on the right. They rocked back and forth on their heels, Lyle smoking and Armand glancing at his wristwatch and adjusting the knot in his tie. That damned elevator moved slowly. When it reached the fourteenth floor, the car stopped and the doors pulled open. A young boy and girl stepped in—nine or ten years old. They were holding hands and they stopped in front of Lyle and Armand and turned their backs to them so they, too, could watch the moving number show above the door.
 When the elevator hit floor twenty–two, the doors once again opened and the couple stepped out. As they did, the boy turned to Lyle and said "You shouldn't smoke in the elevator." And the young lovers ran down the hallway as fast as they could, giggling and holding hands. It was the first time Armand had heard anyone criticize Lyle for his smoking habits.
 The doors closed and the remaining ride was uninterrupted. When the doors re–opened, Lyle and Armand stepped

MINUS 55

into a place they found to be much like the lobby in both coloring and lighting. It was just as silent, too, after the creaky elevator closed and disappeared to another floor.

Locke and Gardetto were in the middle of a hallway. Agent Locke looked at one door and then down to his note pad. Then he proceeded straight left, to room 55C, down at the end of the hall, with Gardetto in tow behind him.

# # #

Agent Locke knocked for the third time on the front door of apartment 55C and he put his specially trained ear to the hinges for a listen—the creak of a floor, water running. He heard nothing.

Lyle had his back to his partner and was looking down the hallway. It was very long. It was a very large building. He alternated between monitoring the way from which he and Armand had come and the other direction the hallway took as it cornered at 55C—to Lyle's right. They were at the corner of a square, 55 stories above the street. It was quiet and the lamps between the apartment doors glowed only for themselves.

"You ready?" Armand asked Lyle.

Lyle swiveled his head around toward his partner. "Nobody home?" We goin' in?" He was whispering.

Agent Locke nodded his head as he reached inside his coat and retrieved a key ring containing three cards—one red, one white, one blue. Locke knelt before the doorknob and examined all of the locks on the door. Then he stood up, slid the blue card into the slot next to the knob. There was a click. Accordingly, the dead bolts clicked as Armand slid the red card into their slots. The door was disengaged.

Lyle took one last look around—behind and to the left. The doors that lined the hall in a staggered fashion were still closed and there was nothing but silence in the air. Not even

ODOM

sounds from the outside made it up that far.

    Agent Locke opened the door and stepped inside—allowed Agent Gardetto to step to the lead, gun drawn. Armand looked down both directions of the hallway and then he shut the door quietly behind him.

    The living room was dark. What a fucking shock, Lyle thought, and he flicked on a floor lamp that stood close to the door when it was swung completely open. There were blankets everywhere. Several were piled up on the couch that lined the wall just to the right of the door. Across from that were more, strewn about a recliner and a love seat.

    Lyle checked the corridor in front of them, but there was nothing coming—no people, no animals, no sounds. He allowed himself to relax a little. He didn't feel any life in the place.

    On the opposite end of the living room, away from the door and the TV, the apartment opened into a little dining area with a small table. To the left of that was the kitchen.

    "Come 'ere," Agent Locke said to Gardetto. "Let's work through from the kitchen."

    It was standard procedure for the man without the gun to examine the specifics—look for anything that might be used as important information— such as notes left behind that gave some idea of the subject's whereabouts, telephone numbers, etc. It was the job of the man with the gun pulled to stand watch over his partner, cover the action, just in case someone had designs on keeping his personals private.

    First, Armand checked out the table in the kitchen. He saw the newspaper and checked the date. There was a pot of coffee on the counter, between the stove and the refrigerator, but it had been turned off. He felt of it and it was cool.

    "There ain't nobody fuckin' here, man," Lyle said and he dropped the gun to his side. He'd been giving a look and listen to

MINUS 55

the back hallway. "We waitin'?"

Armand was still looking around. "Yeah. Yeah, we're definitely waiting." He stood straight and arched his back, let out a sigh. "Let's go ahead and give this place a good once over, though, first."

They left the kitchen and worked their way down the back hallway, which circuitously connected the kitchen to the living room. The apartment was a mini version of the 55th floor. All the living spread out around the framework of a square.

Lyle opened the hallway closet—empty. He walked behind Armand down the hall and checked out the bathroom. He pushed the door open—heard nothing, saw nothing. Armand checked the bedroom, its closet and under the bed, but no one was there, either. It was the same with the second bedroom as well, truly empty.

"Well," Armand said, shutting the door to the spare bedroom, "let's make ourselves at home."

"How long do we wait around?"

"How should I know?"

Armand walked to the front door and looked through the peephole. Everything was still and quiet on the outside. He slid all three of the locks into place. Now they would be forewarned if someone was coming through the door. Then he and his partner made themselves comfortable and waited for their man to arrive.

# # #

Under the bathtub water, Jack was thinking more about his method of attaining breaths than he was about getting the neck manacle off. Every two minutes or so, he would work his face past the surface of the water and exhale the carbon dioxide residuals from the previous breath and refill with the bathroom air. He was keeping his ears underwater at all times so as to

ODOM

adapt—reach a certain level of comfort and ease while he was under the water.

But he wasn't happy with how it was going. He hadn't even considered the chain around his neck in lieu of perfecting the breathing routine. All he could think about was the snorkel he sometimes used during his training.

Slowly, Jack began to raise himself out of the water. He remembered the stitches. They felt OK, numb, but he didn't want to push them and risk any further damage. He stood up knee deep in the water and checked himself over. There was a red ooze coming out of some of the stitched wounds and others were puffy. But they looked alright. He could continue. He stepped out onto the green rug and grabbed a towel off the shelf. He patted himself dry, delicately around the stitches, and he ran the towel across his head once. Then he put the towel around his shoulders, allowing it to hang to his waistline in the back.

His stomach felt tight. It was getting tighter. Jack could taste the whiskey and coffee he'd had for breakfast. He could taste the nap he'd taken earlier in the day. He needed to brush his teeth and get something to eat, but at the moment he felt like doing neither.

"Fuck me," Jack said. He'd felt like this before. It was just like the motion sickness. The kind that rises up in the back of the throat and turns stomachs into knots. Makes it feel like you have to shit, but you don't. There's nothing there. It's a phantom. Jack knew this usually passed without incident as long as he practiced patience and reserved his movements. He made himself a deal—promised he'd eat when his ailing stomach gave him the first chance.

The bathroom door was open enough that Jack didn't have to touch it in order to get out, but he did anyway so he could have some contact with something that was solid. In the hallway he felt weak. He staggered a bit and righted himself by putting his hand on the wall. His thoughts were scattered. He turned the corner to the spare room. As he reached for the doorknob and squeezed it, he heard a voice. He thought it was a figment of his medicated imagination.

"Freeze," said the voice, and Jack turned to see a handgun aiming to part his wet hair. His hands went toward the ceiling, slow and shaking, and the towel around his shoulders fell to his ankles. Now he was naked, the manacle around his neck the only thread.

There were several moments of pause between the three men. Nothing but Jack's stomach moved. As the nausea and desperation reached the top of his throat simultaneously, he began to vomit what fluids were in his belly. They splattered at his feet and on the carpet in front of him, dripped off his chin. Small bits came out in an acidic gush, soft chunks of something or many somethings. The more he thought about them, the more that came, the more he gagged. All naked and wet, he was shivering, trying to keep his hands up.

"Fuckin' Christ!" Agent Gardetto said as he stepped back, thinking for his shoes, into the mouth of the living room. He averted his eyes, but kept his gun on the naked target standing at the door to the spare room.

Agent Locke was expressionless and somewhat relieved—for two reasons, mostly. One, their man was indeed home and, two, he was obviously not armed and visibly unthreatening.

# # #

Jack sat naked on the couch, still damp and still wearing the neck chain. He felt better for the moment, physically, because of his having vomited, but he knew it wouldn't last. It never did. The knots in the stomach and the inevitability of puking always returned. Soon he would feel like shit again. As for the two men now cohabiting his apartment, Jack figured they had some connection to Buddy and that he could just rat out his old pal, if necessary, and then warn him to get out of town and change his name and mode of operations again. Or maybe they were with the NBC in some capacity, pissed off about him ending up naked at the end of his New Year's escape in front of all those families.

Armand kept an eye on Jack and Lyle searched the bathroom for a bathrobe, quickly discovering there was none to be found. There wasn't much of *any*thing in the bathroom, as a matter of fact—no towels, no toilet paper, and the tiniest bar of green soap sitting in the sink. He went to Jack's bedroom, but it was wrecked and he didn't care to go through all of it. So the final decision was that if he didn't find a robe in the spare room, he would just have to tell them that he didn't find anything anywhere. They could find something their goddam selves. He was tired.

The spare bedroom's closet was empty, but in the dresser that sat across from the open trunk, stuffed in the top drawer, was a tightly folded robe. As Lyle started working the folded mass out of the drawer, he recognized immediately that it wasn't a typical bath robe, but that it was something that would remedy their situation. They weren't trying to make the guy look good or anything, they were just trying to sidestep having to look at his dick all afternoon.

Finally, out of tired frustration, Gardetto yanked the stubborn drawer from the dresser, splitting off little slivers of wood in the process, and removed the robe that way. It was like a boxing robe or something, thick and heavy, not thin like a bath robe. It was red and had white and gold stripes running down the sleeves. Lyle held it up in front of him and turned the back around. It read: "Suicide Simmons," blood red letters, the first word stacked upon the second. He liked it a lot, admired it on the way back to the living room.

Jack was grateful, thanked Agent Gardetto as he assumed one should with a gunman being polite, and then he stood up in front of the agents and slowly put the robe over his left arm and then the rest of the way. He grabbed the sides and flapped them in and out, cooling his sick body, and then he wrapped himself up and tied the belt in front, ending the skin show. He sat back down and rubbed his eyes, still feeling dizzy and unsettled—at war with his own body, tentatively allied with hospital medication and alcohol. His hands felt as though he had been using a jackhammer all day. They vibrated and tingled—felt swollen.

Gardetto took to the loveseat. He'd put his gun back in his coat as he was searching for the robe, but now he pulled it out and sat it on the nightstand between he and Armand.

"How are you feeling?" Armand asked.

"Fine," Jack answered without looking at his guests. He was staring into the wall between the lamp and the TV. "Thanks." He crossed his legs and scooted himself back into the crease of the couch. "I will get sick again, though, you know."

"That's all right. Just tell us when."

Jack nodded.

"Actually, Lyle," Armand said, "Why don't you get a trash can or something ready. Something from the kitchen."

Lyle stood up. He disappeared around the corner. He had just been thinking of leaving, remembering Locke's instructions to let him handle this one, only act if necessary. He took his cue and sat down in the kitchen and grabbed one of the whiskey bottles off the table—watched the brown liquid swirl around the bottom and peeled at the label.

Back in the living room, Agent Locke was already beginning his sales pitch—trying to convince Jack to come back to the

ODOM

Bureau with him in order to do a real good thing and save the world. It would be his third attempt of the sort in three days and his act had become polished, if even for the varying materials with which he had to work. He felt comfortable with the whole "end of the world" premise now. He'd been working with it in his mind since the first attempt and thought he had some good ideas for how to get it to really fly.

"Don't be nervous," he said, smooth and easy with the voice. "You can relax. We didn't come up here to harm you in any way. I assure you that."

Jack looked at the gun that Agent Gardetto had left on the coffee table next to Armand, pointing at him, and then he returned his eyes to the wall, TV, and lamp.

"We have actually been sent here to ask a favor of you."

Jack felt the heaviness return to his stomach and he rolled over onto his ride side and curled his legs up toward him, onto the couch. "You're not from the NBC?" he asked with restraint.

Armand laughed. "You think they want to kill you?" he said softly.

"Fuck 'em."

Jack rubbed his hand across his stomach, across the robe fabric that covered it, and he winced. It was hitting him again, coming back quick and sharp—that shit feeling. The knots returned and that taste in his mouth and throat came back with it. He suddenly didn't feel like talking. He needed silence or it was all going to come up again.

"We're actually federal agents. Federal agents from your government," Locke continued, confidently.

Jack nodded, but he wasn't looking at Armand. He wasn't really listening, either. He concentrated on not getting sick again, and on the wall, the table and the window of the dining room.

"Would you like to see my badge?" Armand asked.

MINUS 55

Jack shrugged and shook his head. He sat upright and dropped his head between his knees, held it between his hands and felt the strain build quickly and irreversibly in his guts.

# # #

Lyle was examining the calendar of reasonably naked women on Jack's kitchen wall when he first noticed Armand calling for the trash can. He scrambled around in the kitchen—looked under the sink, in the corners, under the table. Eventually, he had to go into the bathroom to find something serviceable. By the time he reached the living room, Jack had already started heaving. Already, there was a little spot growing on the floor—almost pink, like medicine.

Locke stared, expressionless, at Lyle as he stood across from Jack extending the can to him. He had his fingers folded under his chin. He didn't have to say anything. As Jack got things under control—while he was only dry-heaving—he took the small, aluminum trash can from Lyle. He thanked him.

"Thank..." He said and then he heaved several times, "...you." In between spasms, he took in quick, heavy gasps of air. He was sweating. After 12 or 13 more heaves, the sickness let go of him and Jack relaxed. He blew and spit out the liquid that was left in the corners of his mouth. All that remained was the terrible taste of his stomach.

Armand went to the kitchen and fetched a cup of water, handed it to Jack.

"Whiskey?" Jack asked. Then he laughed feebly at his own joke and spit carelessly toward the trash can.

"Water."

Jack rinsed his mouth out. He took a little sip. "Shit. I hope that's the last of that." He wiped his forehead with the sleeve of his robe. He was shivering.

"You feel alright?" Armand asked. "Better?"

ODOM

Jack nodded. "Better."

Again, Armand stood up. "I tell you what. Let me go down to the car and get something for you—something for that stomach, something that'll make you feel a whole lot better."

Jack nodded. "I need something to eat." He was dipping his fingers into the cup of water, rubbing them across his face and neck. He was leaning back with his eyes closed, shivering all over.

"We can take care of that, too." Armand went to the door and looked through the peephole. It was clear, calm out there in the hallway. He undid the locks and opened the door. When he was outside, the locks clicked again.

"So, you alright?" Lyle asked. "You gonna fucking throw up on us again. You gonna start heaving on us again?" He was laughing. He took his place on the loveseat.

Jack didn't answer. He sat up straight and opened his eyes wide. He took a deep breath through his nose. Then he took another drink of water.

Lyle leaned in and dropped the laugh. "Listen. Before my partner gets back, let me cue you in on a couple things."

Jack moved up the back of the couch, almost straight up, and winced. "I wish you would."

Lyle continued. "When my partner gets back, he's gonna tell you a few things that you're just gonna have to believe. You're just going to have to believe them. Because if you don't, you see, we...we won't have anything here. We can't help you." He held up his hands and shrugged. "He's gonna tell you a lot of things that you may think, at first glance, are completely ridiculous. I mean, to be perfectly honest with you, when I first heard all they had to say about it I thought it was just some unbelievable bullshit. You understand what I'm saying?"

"I thought he said it was some kind of favor he had to

ask." Jack's words were coming through as if he'd just been tossed around, insides and outs.

"It is. Listen to me," Gardetto said. He stood up, picked up the gun off the table, and started to pace back and forth in front of Jack—the coffee table between them. "Just understand that everything this man is going to tell you is the absolute truth. Understand that every word that the man utters will ring true in your ears. And if it doesn't ring true in your ears, do you know what's going to have to happen?"

Jack shook his head.

Lyle stopped in front of him and raised the gun up under his ear like he was shaving his sideburns with the barrel.

"You're gonna to shoot me?"

Lyle was nodding his head, pouting his lips. "Now, I really don't wanna to have to do it, you understand. I don't." He paced and waved the gun around in the air. "What I really want to happen is for you to nod your head and say things like 'Yes sir, Agent Locke,' and 'That makes a great deal of sense to me, Agent Locke.' That's what I want to hear. That's what's gonna make all this real, real easy. Do you understand what I'm saying?"

Jack sat still. His stomach knotted again—pulled up from the bottom, but it wasn't the sickness coming back. He was nervous. There had been times not so far removed when Jack had considered the positive aspects of an untimely demise, but at the moment, with a gunman in the room (although he seemed as reasonable as they must come), Jack wanted to live. Going out on someone else's whim just didn't hold the same appeal. He could live with a sort of death that was self-perpetuated—drinking too much, smoking too much, not escaping from an underwater escape too much. In his business, there was something immortalizing about all of that—self-perpetuating. He could have that. His inevitable, last moments could be fine ones. It was a part of

ODOM

his whole shtick. It *was* his shtick.

"I get it, man," Jack responded, self-perpetuating. He had his palms up in front of himself. "I get it. I can't see why I'd give you guys any problems."

Gardetto put the gun back in the holster under his arm. He took his jacket off and tossed it in the loveseat. He loosened his blue and white striped tie and took a deep breath. "Fuckin' hot," he said.

Jack nodded. Lyle's shirt was baggy, but sticking to him in places. He was a pretty big guy, a little bigger than Jack. His shoulders were a lot wider. His hair, which had once been slicked back, was starting to rise like an arc-sprinkler coming back across a yard.

"Yeah, so where the hell were you when we came in?" Lyle asked and sat back down on the loveseat. "Where the hell did you come from?"

"I was in the tub...under the water," Jack answered and he pulled at the neck chain.

"That's a professional thing?"

Jack nodded. He glanced at the door, expected it to be opening at any time.

"Can't you get it off?"

"No."

"Why not?"

"I don't know."

Lyle shook his head. "I don't understand."

"Neither do I," Jack answered. He felt more comfortable in this topic of conversation than he had in the "untimely death" one, and his stomach began to settle. However, he kept an ear on the door, eager for the small guy to return. "I've got some picks in the kitchen. I can get it off if I've got a pick." Jack was trying to trick the big guy into giving him a few seconds to disappear into.

"In the kitchen?" Lyle asked and pointed to the kitchen entrance.

Jack nodded.

"When Agent Locke gets back, I'll get you a pick."

Jack took another sip from the cup of water sitting on the coffee table in front of him. He cleared his throat and spit some orange–yellow into the can. He considered time and decided he should start trying to buy some. "So, you have a name?" he asked.

"Gardetto."

"Gardetto." Again, he spit. "Is that right?" A deep breath and a drink. "When I was a kid...my dad drove a delivery truck for a warehouse, like a grocery warehouse or something. He used to bring us shit home sometimes—extra shit that nobody needed...That's what he used to tell us. Sometimes...he'd bring home these little bags of snacks, kind of like trail mix or something, called 'Gardetto's' ...That was the name of them, 'Gardetto's.'"

Lyle nodded. "Yeah."

The locks clicked and Armand returned.

# # #

Jack chewed the toast and jelly and worked at the lock constricting his neck with the pick Gardetto had brought him. Lyle retreated to the kitchen, back to the hypnotic gaze of the All–American calendar.

"The pills I gave you should make your stomach feel better almost immediately," Locke said and he retook his place in the living room.

"All of them?" Jack said.

"Two. That third one's to take the edge off a little, bring you around."

The neck chain came off and Jack tossed it to the floor to

the right of the coffee table. He rubbed his neck and twisted his head. Armand gave him some time—time for the toast and some for working the neck.

"Everything alright, now?" Armand asked. "Are we feeling well enough to continue our discussion?"

Jack took another bite of the toast and took a look at the kitchen entrance. He laughed a little at the question. "I guess."

"OK...OK, we're not from the NBC, we're from the government. We're federal agents. We've established that, correct?"

Jack nodded. His stomach felt good, like it had been lined with a layer of morphine. He was relaxed and more alert than he'd been since he'd been on the platform, above that tank of water. The better feelings came to him in waves.

"Good," Armand said and he crossed his legs, lined up the crease in his pants with the center of his knee and recognized that the gun from the table to his left was gone.

Jack finished off his two pieces of toast and some more of the water. He felt replenished, rejuvenated by the toast and water, and the pills. Those pills. He felt like having a drink and a cigarette.

Armand folded his hands in his lap. "As I said earlier, my partner and I are here to ask a favor of you. Not on our behalf, really, but on behalf of every person in this country and in fact, the entire world."

Jack nodded and smiled. What is this guy talking about, he thought.

"But before I explain the specifics of the favor to you, let me first explain the situation we are dealing with at the moment," Armand continued, and he stood up from the chair and reached inside the breast of his coat. He retrieved a leather wallet and opened it up in front of himself with one hand. He placed it on the coffee table, between the saucer full of crumbs and jelly, and the empty cup of water.

Jack looked it over. It was gold and not unlike the shield of a police badge. It had the initials "B.A.D." large across the top and then a number at the bottom that read "127".

"What's B.A.D.?" Jack asked.

"It stands for Bureau of Astronomical Destruction."

Jack nodded and then started to shake his head. "I've never heard of that. You say you're with the *fed*eral government?"

Locke smiled a tired smile. "I understand. The fact of the matter is that no one outside the federal government, and in fact, very few people on the inside of the federal government know we exist."

Again, Jack nodded. He'd always suspected there were things of which he knew absolutely nothing about.

"We at the Bureau—people like Agent Gardetto and myself—are concerned with the goings–on of extra terrestrial bodies that have the potential of causing negative changes for the earth and its inhabitants," Locke said.

Jack looked back down at the badge. It was polished, almost glowing.

Armand sat back down and went right into his story. Enough time had been wasted. He informed Jack of the enormous, "Super–Massive" asteroid that was perilously headed for the earth. He told him that the Super–Massive was nearly ten miles in diameter while the one that wiped out the dinosaurs was an estimated six miles across. Actually, he told him it was only five, having whittled it down from the first telling.

As the story rattled on, Jack put his hands on top of his head and leaned back into the couch. His hair was still a bit wet. He felt as if he was watching Armand on film, an actor in front of him. He looked back and forth between the TV and Agent Locke. "OK," Jack said and he leaned back in towards the coffee table.

ODOM

"Alright."

"This asteroid is coming at us, you see." Armand illustrated with his closed fists, one symbolizing the earth and the other playing the asteroid. He was cooking. "And when it hits..." He paused a great pause and held onto his breath for effect. Then, he launched conclusively, "Everybody dies. Most of it won't take much longer than a few minutes, almost instantaneously for most. But some life will linger and die out more slowly—starving and freezing, you see. It's no way to go, I assure you." Then Armand stopped and gave Jack plenty of room to respond. He wanted to sweep him up, get him going, and then get his ass in the car. He was wearing down.

Jack took a long breath and blew it all out. He shook his head. "I...damn, man...I don't know." He rubbed his hand on his head, messing his hair. He laughed a little. "This sounds like a lot of crazy...it's craziness...you know, man. I mean, I don't mean to offend you or anything, but this sounds like some crazy bullshit."

Agent Locke looked surprised and for a moment he deflated. His eyebrows went down into his eyes and his forehead wrinkled down into the eyebrows as he examined the gutless, anti–patriot, worm that sat across from him. He was growing more fatigued by the second. "What's wrong?" he asked and laughed exasperatedly.

Jack was still shaking his head. He wasn't sure what to say and he stammered out some words, started and stopped several times. "Man, if you were seein' this from where I'm seein' it…" he said and slapped the couch cushion. And things did look different—they were brighter, more engaged with the senses.

Armand was back to having his legs crossed. He smiled again. He really wanted to pull this one together, failure not being a viable option. "You're right," he said. "You get out of the bathtub just after practicing your little escape or something, am I right? Did I hear that right?"

"Right. That's right."

"And two guys in matching suits break into your apartment and stick a gun to your head, am I right?" Armand continued, getting louder. He was building steam again, if in another direction. "Then you throw up all over the place, we tell you we're from the government and then I start telling you giant asteroid stories, is that right?"

Jack was nodding. His mouth was open in a kind of smile as he imagined the laughter of an invisible audience.

"I think I understand. I do," Agent Locke said. "We could be simple thugs, right? Am I right? Simple thugs who get their kicks from telling their victims big ole bullshit stories like the one I've been telling you. In fact, we might do this sort of thing all the time, right—go into someone's home and lay on a thick story, pull out a badge, flash a gun and then blow their brains out right after we've had our daily fun. Right? Am I right?" Jack's smile fell from his mouth like a long-rotting tooth. Armand continued. "Really, there, Mr. Suicide, I can understand how you must feel."

Armand was shaking his head. He drew a deep breath and let it out slowly. "Lyle," he called to the kitchen. No answer. "Lyle!" A few moments later Lyle came around the corner. He was eating a piece of toast.

"Agent Gardetto," Locke said looking up at him from the recliner. "Mr. Simmons isn't ready to listen to my story. It seems as though he suffers from a lack of attention.

Jack was squirming. He was confused, felt like a small kid about to be taken down a notch by the neighborhood bullies.

"This isn't going to work out," Armand said, exhausted. "I'm afraid we'll have to find someone else."

ODOM

Lyle sat the half–eaten piece of toast on the table next to Armand. He reached under his arm and slid his weapon out of the leather shoulder holster like he was sliding it out of a woman. Jack saw it all happening in slow motion—a 3–D movie sequence.

Agent Gardetto extended his arm, locked his elbow and locked his gun sights on the middle of Jack's forehead.

"I'm ready to go whenever you are, Lyle," Armand said. He was examining his fingernails.

Jack couldn't speak. He didn't know what was going on, didn't know what to say. He managed to mutter a "stop" just as Lyle squeezed the trigger. Jack started to close his eyes. His head was pounding like a bass drum as the blood rushed through his brain, feeling the bullet before it left the chamber.

The gun clicked, but that was it. Lyle dropped the gun to his side. Jack exhaled and started breathing again, sweating again.

Gardetto put the gun back in the holster and picked his coat up off the loveseat. He popped the remaining piece of toast into his mouth and put the coat back on.

Jack clenched the front of his robe, flapped it in and out to cool himself.

Lyle disappeared into the kitchen, reappearing seconds later with another plate of toast and another cup of water for Jack. He took the empty cup and empty saucer back to the kitchen and then sat at the table reloading his empty weapon.

#

"Would you mind it so much if I got a drink?" Jack asked. "You see, I'm a drinker and...now seems like no time for me to be quittin'." He laughed.

Armand smiled. Jack was tapping his heels against the floor and chewing on his right thumbnail. His hair was almost dry now, stiff towards the back and turning back into brown from the wet black. He was still wired and vibrating, still flying.

MINUS 55

"I don't suppose that's a problem," Armand answered. "Lyle. Could you fix Mr. Simmons a drink?"

"Just bring me the bottle and a cup if you don't mind, there, Lyle," Jack added loudly. He checked Armand to see if he was still smiling and he was, like it was stuck in that position. After a moment, he could hear Lyle mulling about the kitchen.

"This alright?" he asked Armand as he rounded the corner into the living room. He raised the bottle and the cup when he spoke, exposing the gun under his arm to Jack.

Agent Locke confirmed by nodding his head once. He really looked in control, Jack thought. He looked confident. Jack needed that drink to level the playing field. "Thanks," Jack said and Lyle sat the bottle and cup on the table in front of him.

Jack spun the brown cap off the bottle of brown liquid and poured himself half a cup. He mixed some of the water from the other cup in with the whiskey and knocked back a gulp. The first straight one of the day always made Jack think of gasoline, fuel. He had another drink, washed it around in his mouth, and sat the cup back on the table. Lyle returned to the kitchen, backstage.

Agent Locke looked at his watch. He looked for a long time, long enough for Jack to have a couple more quick drinks. Then he pulled his briefcase from beside his chair. Jack hadn't noticed this before and he expected to see another gun come out of it. This was getting ridiculous, he thought. Guns, guns, guns.

But there was no gun. Armand opened the case in his lap and began punching the keys as he seemed so fond of doing. He was quick, flipping from one screen to the next, one file to another. Jack watched intently, taking sips of his drink as he looked on. After several single key strokes, Agent Locke sat back in his chair and stared at the screen. He glanced at Jack and Jack looked down into the cup he was holding between his fingertips.

ODOM

A piece of paper accompanied by a sound that Jack was unfamiliar with began rising behind the propped open back of the black case. Jack sat forward on the couch. Things were stranger and stranger and the whiskey helped keep Jack in his skin.

"I want you to take a good look at this, Mr. Simmons," Armand said and he pulled the paper free from the machine and placed the machine, still open, on the ground. He stood up and leaned the print toward Jack. He really felt he had this one in the bag.

On the paper Jack saw a beautiful woman with black hair streaked with brown, pulled back behind her ear on one side. Her skin was pure and brown, untanned by the sun, and her eyes were wide open and taking in everything. It looked exactly the same as the picture trapped beneath Jack's stove.

Jack's eyes began to water like he'd just been punched on the nose and he forgot, for a moment, to breathe. It seemed like it had been years since he'd seen Sarah, not even that picture, and at times he couldn't even remember what she looked like as he tried to put her together in his mind.

"How did you get this?" Jack asked Agent Locke, looking up from the picture.

"I get whatever I want," Armand said coldly, straight and sharp.

"What do you know about her?"

"Whatever I want."

Again, Jack looked at the picture. He closed his eyes and took a deep breath, sure now that he was riding in a current beyond his control and comprehension. "How does she fit into this?"

"If you don't come with us, Jack, she's gonna die right along with you —one way or another," Armand answered. "Either, you stay here and die *and* she dies or you go with us and she lives. That's it. That's all there is to it."

"Some kinda deal," Jack said, but he held onto his frustrated confusion.

Armand nodded. He was tired. But still sticking to his story. "That's how it all works out."

Jack started to ask some questions but decided they weren't very good ones. He looked away from Armand so he could think, but he couldn't get it going except to promise himself some thoughts at the first moment that presented clarity. Armand's wasn't really much of a compromise, though. This he realized. He didn't know what to do beyond going along, buying more time until he could figure things out.

When all was said and things settled in a little, Jack told Agent Locke he'd do it for Sarah.

Buying time. Buying time.

ODOM

"B.A.D."

From the back seat of the Buick, Jack could see the rain clouds gather above the green trees and begin relieving themselves on the hills in the distance. The city was gone. The apartment was gone. All Jack had with him—besides the sweatpants, T–shirt, and gym shoes he was wearing—was a cardboard box containing his cigarettes, two bottles of whiskey, and a couple pairs of fresh underwear that were wrapped in and around the bottles to keep them from clinking together.

Lyle and Armand were sitting up front, Armand driving and Lyle smoking the obligatory cigarette. Now, usually when the agents were bringing in a subject, Lyle would ride in the back seat with the newest addition, but Lyle had decided that Jack still didn't "look so good" and he didn't want him "barfing on" him. So, because of that and the fact that both agents considered a vomiting, drugged man who had recently been released from the hospital because of a horribly botched underwater escape to be sufficiently submissive, they let him ride alone in the back seat. It was all his to throw up in.

As the car bounced down the highway, Armand struggling against the elements to keep them off the shoulder and on their side of the center line, Jack laid down in the back seat. He'd had enough of looking out his window—enough with all that damned grass and all that distance. There was no question that the rain would eventually reach them, no question that looking across all that damned expanse would soon become strained. He stretched out in the back seat as best he could, and tried to move himself with the motion of the car, tried to keep his head from spinning too much.

"We're gonna get it," Armand said. "It's really blowin'."

"Just keep us on the road," said Lyle behind a puff of smoke.

The car would go left and then right with the gusts of wind and Armand's compensations. It was a bad ride and Jack started to get queasy again. He pulled a newspaper off the floorboard from underneath his box of goodies and folded it over thick so he could use it as a pillow. He pulled his shirt up over his belly and wiped his face with it. Several days of stubble had overrun the smooth skin on his face, stretched from ear to ear and in under his nose like a bandana mask. Although he'd gotten out of the bathtub only a couple hours earlier, Jack felt dirty. He needed a shower. He needed to wash his face.

The Buick started up a small hill and the wind on top was more forceful. It was getting darker and darker as the black and blue giants extended over the entire countryside like a retractable ceiling. It was like they were being shut in, all closed up.

When the rain came Jack decided he'd just go ahead and vomit. What the hell did it matter? He opened up the newspaper and began working it into the shape of a bowl or something passable, and he tried to make it as thick as possible. When it didn't work out, he threw up in his hand.

# # #

Between obscenities Lyle informed Armand that there was a diner just over the next hill where they could stop for awhile and "get all that shit cleaned up." Armand was still at war, he with the Buick, against the powers of nature. The car continued to bounce and move erratically from side to side. The stretches in between the small hills were bad because there was already water settling there. On the inclines the wind was worse. With his head down into the newspaper, Jack couldn't tell the difference. From where he was sitting, all there was was that smell—newspaper soaked with vomit.

The car made it up the next hill and the spasms in Jack's body paused long enough to allow him to look up. Lyle looked back at him disgustedly and then down to the newspaper. Jack started to say something to him but he stopped himself and spit into the paper.

"It's right up ahead," Lyle said and he pointed ahead and to his right. There was the glow from a sign out front but the words on it weren't visible, obscured by the downpour. Armand pulled them in and parked the car in the middle of the small lot.

"OK," Armand sighed. He was relieved to be sitting still. "Alright, I'll go in and get some rags or something, a trash can, something, and we'll get this taken care of." He looked to Lyle but Lyle was looking out his window. "Sit tight," Armand said and he was out into the rain, slamming his door, sprinting and disappearing into the diner.

Lyle turned around toward Jack. He looked at the ruined newspaper and at Jack's box of personals. "Why didn't you throw up in that fuckin' box?"

"It's my box," Jack said, and he wiped his mouth. "It's all I've got."

"It woulda been fuckin' cleaner. We coulda just tossed it out and gone on. Look at the fuckin' mess! It's all over the goddam floorboard."

Some had gotten on the seat and some was on Jack's hand, but most of it was on the paper. Lyle was overreacting. Even the misfires Jack had corralled onto the newspaper. He'd always fancied himself a clean retcher and, all things considered, he felt this was an instance of pretty clean retching.

"Shut up," Jack said, interrupting Lyle's tirade.

Lyle looked quizzically at Jack. "What?"

Jack unlocked the door on the driver's side of the backseat and he got rid of the paper as well as most of the vomit. The rain fell hard and popped the paper until it was thoroughly soaked. The water was also splashing into the back seat some, enough for Jack to clean his hands and wash his face, get his hair damp again. It felt real good. He needed it. He thought about getting out and standing in it, thought about making an angry dash for the hills, but it would have been fruitless. He had no fantasies about getting shot in the back of his head.

When he closed the door, Lyle was still looking at him.

"You ever throw up?" Jack asked.

Lyle didn't follow.

"You ever throw up?"

Lyle cocked a smile. "Of course. But not since I was a kid."

Jack nodded. His hands were shaking again as he wiped his nose, but he felt good, the gift of his purging. "I suppose…that when you threw up…you did a lot of talkin'?"

Lyle didn't follow.

"That's why I said 'shut up.'"

"Why?"

Jack shook his head.

Lyle shook his head. He was going to say something else, but he stopped short. He lit a cigarette instead. He gave one to Jack.

When Armand returned he was carrying coffee and some muffins, had a bunch of rags and napkins stuffed in his pockets. The rain was slowing and the smell of vomit was being pushed aside by the cigarette smoke.

# # #

ODOM

Jack had a blueberry muffin, but it didn't last. He took it down in only a couple bites, partially filling the emptiness in his stomach. He imagined an ulcer growing down there. He imagined the blueberries in the muffin coating the bleeding ulcer with purple, like good medicine would. It made him feel better—took his mind off his situation. He just closed his eyes and thought blueberries.

The coffee was bland, like slightly flavored water, so Jack mixed a little whiskey with it as soon as he drank enough to get plenty in. Armand and Lyle took their time with their muffins and coffee. It was like they rarely ate and so enjoyed each morsel of nourishment as if it might be their last.

The rain was slowing up as suddenly as it had come and Jack noticed, for the first time, the name of the diner on the sign out front—the one which he had seen glowing behind the downpour. It read "Last Stop Eat and Run." He'd never heard of it.

"That's supposed to be the last of the rain for awhile," Armand said, swallowing some coffee.

"Yeah. It'll probably be snowin' tomorrow," Lyle said.

Armand looked in the rear view mirror at Jack. "You feeling better?" he asked.

"I guess."

"I see you got everything cleaned up back there, huh?"

Jack nodded and sipped some coffee.

A car pulled up to the first row of the parking lot, right in front of the diner, and a family got out. There were parents and a couple kids, a grandmother. Jack watched them, looking through the windshield, between Lyle and Armand. The kids were running around, chasing each other through the puddles the storm had left behind for them. The parents were helping the grandmother out of the front seat of the car. It was so ordinary, Jack felt like he should cry.

But he didn't cry. And he didn't look away, either, although he felt like doing that as well. He watched them all the way into the diner, watched the jingling door ease shut behind the mother as she corralled her children in before her. Jack put a little more whiskey in his coffee.

"Jack."

"What?"

Armand turned around in his seat to face Jack. "Can you tell me how you're feeling? I mean, do you still feel the effects of the medicine I gave you?"

Jack thought it in for a second. "No. I feel regular, I guess."

Armand nodded. "Alright. We need to get you a little more, then."

Lyle finished his coffee and crushed his cup at his feet. "You can't keep throwin' up, though, you know," he said. "It's not gonna do you much good if you keep throwin' the shit up."

"You say you feel pretty good, aye?" Armand asked again.

"I'm good."

Armand got out of the car and went around to the trunk, which was already opening. When he came back, he had three pills which looked identical to the first three Jack had taken.

"I need some more coffee to wash these down," Jack said. "I'm almost dry." He drank the rest.

"OK. I'll get another round of everything, then."

Armand shut the door and went back to the diner.

"I don't wanna give you crazy–asses any reason to shove these things up my ass, you know what I mean," Jack said to Lyle, looking out his window and holding the pills extended in his palm. He took in some smoke.

Lyle shook his head. "You'd just get the shits."

# # #

ODOM

Armand pulled the car from the parking lot and put it back on the open road, wide open. Jack spilled his new cup of coffee a little as they went over a bump, spilled it down his chin. It was hot. It felt good. The second muffin Armand had brought back for Jack, another blueberry one, was even better than the first—like it had come straight from the box.

Once the coffee cooled down, Jack took the three pills he had been given. They left a sticky spot on his palm and he tried to lick it clean, tried getting all he could. It tasted awful.

"About an hour, you say?" Armand asked Lyle.

"Nah, not quite. Forty–five minutes, maybe," Lyle answered. "Maybe a little less."

Jack assumed they were talking about how long it was going to take to get wherever it was they were taking him. He thought about asking where they were heading, but he didn't. Instead, he yawned and lit a cigarette. He took long, slow drags and exhaled just as slowly through his nose. He yawned again to try to pop his ears, but the more air he took in the fuller his ears became until it sounded like he was underwater again. He closed his eyes. He couldn't tell if someone in the front seat was talking or it was just the sound of the tire tread surfing the wet highway. Or maybe it was the windshield wipers slapping back and forth metronomically along the glass. He took another long drag off his smoke.

Jack's eyes opened and closed slowly and over and over, in sync with the grey rolling out of his nose like the barrel of a gun. He could feel himself slowing down. His blinking made noise on the inside of his head, like doors slamming shut in a library.

The car began to slow down and Jack struggled to keep his balance as Armand turned the car left, the first turn since the diner. The sun was now to the left of the car, or at least the illuminated, orange clouds that cloaked the sun. Jack watched them as they moved, tried to stare at them for fear of closing his eyes. He half–believed he was dying right there in the back of that goddamned Buick. He thought that if he could just keep an eye open he could fight it off, rebound and pull himself out of it. But his confidence was slipping.

They drove for several more miles until they reached a high fence, electrically charged (according to the sign) and topped with great loops of razor wire. Jack noticed a booth to the left. There was a man inside.

A loud static came into the car, like phone line static with a few beeps and hums buried inside it. When it stopped, Armand took something out of his pocket and inserted it somewhere underneath the steering wheel. A few moments later, there came a wave from inside the booth.

The gate in front of them opened and Armand took the Buick through. There was another gate and then some more still, until five had opened in front of them—all electrically charged (according to the signs) and topped with great loops of razor wire. As the Buick moved past the gates, each one closed and buzzed behind them. After the fifth closed and buzzed, there were no more gates, just more open road.

The gates and the booth and the man in the booth were the first concrete inklings to Jack that Lyle and Armand had been telling him the truth about why they needed him. Not to mention the razor wire and the signs. Jack believed for the first time that he might actually be headed for some martyr–like date with death. It made him feel lonely, heading toward absolutely nothing— especially with the lack of publicity. He could never really grasp the concept of dying, of absolutely nothing for absolutely forever. It didn't seem like any kind of reality to him. He wanted out of that back seat, wanted to make a break for it, but it was too

ODOM

late for that kind of thinking. Any movement would have caused his rigid body, leaning hard to the left, to collapse into the back seat.

I'm a goddamned man, Jack thought, a goddamned man.

# # #

"I'm a goddamned man," Jack said. He was surprised to hear anything come out of his mouth.

Lyle turned and looked around the back of his seat. He had a perplexed look on his face. "You say something?"

No.

Lyle smiled and wiped some drool off Jack's chin with one of the rags Armand had brought back from the diner. "Just relax Jack. Sit back and think about that pretty girl or something. Enjoy the ride, baby."

So Jack thought about Sarah. He leaned left and thought about that pretty girl. He wondered if she was goddamned, too. Thinking about her reminded him *why* he was where he was. He was a hero for her. He seemed to remember something about that. Even if he was drooling and leaning hopelessly left.

A large, rectangular mass of trees appeared to the left and Armand turned the car down another road, toward them. It was almost dark, the orange clouds losing their power, and the clump of trees standing in the middle of the flatland looked like a black building, an ominous shadow extending from it, greeting them.

As the dense mass grew closer, the shadows grew longer and covered the car with a blanket of premature night. The sun was gone.

Armand pushed a button on the dashboard and the headlights came on. At last count for Jack, the Buick entered the black building and took one continuous turn, corkscrewing to the left, into some unknown quantity at the center. The centripetal force leveled him out in the back seat, comfortable enough to

MINUS 55

allow him to succumb to sleep after he'd adjusted his stitched body into comfort with the last of his quickly fading energy.

ODOM

"Slow Sedation"

After the concentric maze that led to the underground labyrinth that was the B.A.D., Armand pulled the car into the garage and docked it next to the front door. Two very large men in white suits carried Jack from the Buick's back seat to a room on the second floor, floor "B"—one that had been designated for him. Once inside, the white–clad men strapped Jack to the bed and covered him with a heavy, red blanket. It was cool in there, like an operating room, and seemed sterile like one as well. As the two gentlemen left Jack alone to sleep, one of them dimmed the lights and the other said they were dimmed just enough.

Lyle and Armand had rooms as well—rooms without straps on the beds—and they headed for them in order to get a little rest. It was to be the first horizontal sleep they had had in days.

# # #

After Armand's nap, he got out of bed and showered and shaved. He put on a new suit of clothes and headed to Information with his computer briefcase.

"Hello, Agent Locke," said the lady in Information. She wore a navy blue suit, very professional. When she smiled, Armand smiled.

"Hi."

The Information Agent took the briefcase from Armand and sat it behind her on a counter. "Is there anything you need to tell us?" she asked.

"No. It's all in there."

She nodded. "You sound pretty tired."

"Yeah. Had a little field work."

She handed Armand another briefcase and smiled. "Well, you're finished here if we don't need to get anything else from you."

"Good. Thanks." Armand took the briefcase and returned the smile. When he got to the door, he stopped and turned back around. "Agent Roberts?" he asked as the woman was disappearing into the room beyond the counter.

She stopped. "Yes?"

"Where's the closest cup of coffee on this level?"

She smiled. "Down the hall to the right. First door."

"Thanks."

# # #

Armand headed for a couple cups of the good coffee. Level C housed the Information Department as well as the Experimental Labs, but most people thought of it as the floor with the good coffee. Level A was the security level, where most of the monitoring and outside communications were handled—terrible coffee. Level B was the housing level—average coffee, but lots of it. And level D was the supplies floor and it also connected the core building with all of its peripheries—no coffee at all unless you dragged a maker down there yourself.

It had been rumored that one of the lab people had found or created an additive that was put in the C level coffee, but it had never been confirmed. When Armand got to the lounge area, Lyle was already sitting at one of the tables.

"Get any sleep?" Lyle asked as Armand took a seat across from him.

"Yeah. You?"

"A little." They had to speak loudly. There were several

ODOM

people in the lounge, talking, taking breaks. It was more like a high school cafeteria than a lounge, really—in order to accommodate the large numbers that were to use it.

Armand sipped his coffee. "Good coffee."

"Hot."

Armand nodded.

Sometimes they didn't have a great deal to say to each other, especially if they had been out for an extended period of time. They had grown accustomed to sitting in one another's silence. After a few minutes, however, Lyle spoke.

"How do you feel about everything?" he said.

"Fine. It's going well, I think." Armand shrugged his shoulders, puffed out his cheeks with coffee. "I think he might make it," he said.

Lyle shrugged his shoulders and hunched around his coffee mug. "I guess you took the computer to information?"

Locke nodded.

Lyle checked his watch and ran his fingers through his hair. "Well, I tell you what. I'm gonna fill up here and go on upstairs and take a shower, get a shit in, have a shave, a cigarette, and then I'll meet you in our boy's room. How's about that?"

"Yeah," Armand said. "That sounds fine. I'll meet you up there in, say," he looked at his watch, "half an hour?"

"Good."

Lyle left.

# # #

Lyle showed up in a new suit of clothes and a freshly shaved face. Armand was in a chair sitting next to Jack, who was still asleep, still on his back and strapped to the cot.

"He's still out?" Lyle said.

"Yeah. Well, he was up just a minute ago. They came in and got the samples from him," Armand answered, referring to the two lab technicians that had been there when Armand arrived.

"Was he coherent?"

Armand laughed. "More or less. They asked him for a stool sample and he told 'em they could go ahead and take the whole thing."

Lyle took a seat.

"They told me to wait a few minutes and then wake him up again, give him this." It was another pill.

"What's that one for?" Lyle asked.

"Alertness. They need to take him down to one of the labs for a couple final tests," Armand said.

"Why do they have to take him down?"

Armand shrugged. "I don't know, really. Probably for some kind of observation. Or maybe they just have some equipment down there that they can't bring up here. Maybe just for show, who knows?"

Gardetto nodded. He looked at Jack. He looked a lot different lying still the way he was. It was quite a contrast to his adventures in the back of the Buick. The red blanket that stretched across him rose and fell with the evenness of his breathing and there was just a hint of a snore reverberating from the back of his throat. It would be a pity to wake him.

"Hey, listen," Armand said and he handed Lyle the pill. "I'm gonna go use the bathroom and grab another cup of coffee. Can you stay here and give him this if he should wake up? There's a little water over there."

"Sure," Lyle answered. Armand was heading for the door. "Bring me another cup, too."

# # #

Lyle woke Jack up by shaking his shoulders a little and blowing a little smoke in his face.

ODOM

"Mister Suicide," he said slowly, blew some smoke. "Mister Suicide." Jack came around with a gasp that he sucked in and choked on.

"Relax," Lyle said. Then he sat back down and returned his focus to his cigarette, which was burning in the ashtray on the table next to the bed.

Jack noticed the strap across his waist and the one across his ankles. He felt like he was at work. "What's this?" he asked Lyle, his lips and tongue numb.

"Ah, that's nothing," Lyle answered. "Just to keep you on the bed and all. In the safety zone."

Jack filed through his memory and it came back chronologically from his apartment. He remembered the car and the rain, remembered why his mouth tasted like warm shit water. He remembered the ride through the countryside. The rest of the story, however, up to Jack's present, was based solely on educated assumption.

Jack lifted his head off the pillow to give a look around. There wasn't much to see—just a couple chairs, one occupied by the smoking Lyle, and the bed he was lying in. His box of personals was next to the door. Jack felt a twinge of compassion when he looked at it. Just a box sitting next to a door, autonomous, overflowing with whiskey bottles and underpants. It seemed like innocence.

Jack's head went back to the pillow and settled in. He took a deep breath. "These straps..." he said.

"Yeah," Lyle interrupted, and he stood up from his seat. "We can take those off now." He worked on the first for a few seconds and then unlatched it, threw it over the bed and onto the floor. Then he undid the one at the foot of the bed.

"Just relax," Lyle continued. "Here, have a little water."

Lyle got Jack some water and Jack sat up against the metal

headboard. He was disoriented, but more than that he was thirsty. "Thanks."

"Take this."

Lyle put the pill in front of Jack and Jack took it from his palm. He thought about it for a second, and then popped it in his mouth and began washing it down. It was funny, the kind of trust that had been developed between Jack and the agents. It was trust based, from Jack's perspective, on the simple fact that he was still alive, that they hadn't shot him at his apartment or killed him somewhere in the middle of all those miles of countryside. It was trust based on the negative, faith that was blind.

"You think I..." Jack said and he locked his eyes on Lyle's cigarette. He motioned with his hand.

Lyle deciphered the charade and pulled his pack out of an inside, coat pocket. "Sure, man. Here you go."

# # #

By the end of Jack's cigarette, the pill he had taken was beginning to blossom inside his stomach. He started to feel that his skin was moving over his bones. When Armand came into the room, Jack had a brief, splitting notion of excitement that produced little beads of sweat on his forehead and upper lip.

"Up, already? Good." He handed Lyle a cup of coffee. "Did you do the pill, already?" he asked him under his breath.

Lyle nodded.

Armand left the room and returned before the door swung shut. He pushed a wheelchair in front of him.

A goddamned wheelchair, Jack thought. But he couldn't take his eyes off it. He wanted to climb into it. He wanted to go spinning down the hall, roaring down the hall on the hard rubber tires. He wanted to rest his cold feet in the steel trays that were made for them, to feel the air rushing between his toes. He wanted to take that sad box that sat motionless next to the door as well,

ODOM

wanted it riding in his lap. Jesus Christ, yes!, he thought.

"Wanna take a quick little ride with us, Jack?" Armand said. "To another room for awhile?"

Jack tingled as the pill reverberated through his every sense. His whole body began to perspire and he laughed a couple short bursts. Then he said, in a soft, timid voice that cracked, "Jesus Christ, yes."

MINUS 55

"A Lobotomy and a Chest X-ray"

The next room was a little smaller, a medical examination room, and had three little, clear containers and one big one sitting on a long counter that ran in front of one of the walls. One container held a mixture of blood and something that had been added to it by one of the two technicians that was working on and around Jack. The other small containers had the same secret ingredient added to urine and saliva. All fluids were Jack's.

The larger container had been the most enjoyable for Jack to fill—the stool sample pan. It was the first relief he'd seen in days. This container also had the secret additive as well as another spoonful of stuff that looked like taco seasoning—most assuredly something that smelled nice or negated anything that didn't.

The technicians were busy studying charts and turning on machines and manipulating machines and all the things technicians are supposedly supposed to do. They were both males. In fact, Jack believed, had he not seen them together, he would have thought them to be the *same* male. They weren't twins by any means, but they were equally generic, like products from exactly similar assembly lines. Jack folded up little pieces of paper from the sheet beneath him and flicked them at the men to watch them fall to the floor.

Occasionally, one of the men disappeared into another room—one with a large, metal door closing off any view of the inside. They took turns, flicking switches and then vanishing

ODOM

into this other room. Before long they were taking the samples, one after another, with them past the metal door until only the large container remained. Then they were both back and working at the controls again.
"Go ahead."
"Right now?"
"Yeah. Go ahead."
One of the technicians, the one who was exactly as tall as the other one and with the same wavy hair, approached Jack and smiled at him. He extended a paper disc with a pill sitting on top of it. In his other hand, he had a small cup of water, half–filled.
"Here you go," he said.
"What is it?"
"It's a pill. Just something we need you to take before we get the last test from you."
That didn't sound very good to Jack, "get the last test from you," but it didn't really matter. He didn't really care. He took the pill, washed it down, and then wadded up the paper disc in his fingertips and flicked it off the top of the plastic jar containing his very own shit sample.

# # #

The paper started to feel bad between Jack's fingers as he contemplated more paper wad throwing and rubbed the torn sheet with his hand. His fingertips felt coarse and numb, like the cool, plastic pad underneath the paper was creeping up through him and the floor vents were seeping cool breezes in his direction. The perspiration was still there. His hairs stood on end, goosebumps supporting them like little flagpoles.
"Why dontcha go ahead and lie back on the table there, Mr. Simmons," said Technician number one or two.
"Jack."
"Yes."

MINUS 55

The man helped Jack's shoulders back onto the padded paper. It felt awfully unforgiving and hard, like there had to be concrete underneath.

Jack took a deep breath and wiped his forehead with the front of his shirt. Then he sat up on his elbows to keep an eye on what was going on.

Finally, the stool sample was being taken away. Jack had been worried that he was going to be the only one who got to partake in its glorious splendor and pleasure–giving qualities. He wiped his forehead.

"Just lie back," someone said and then they, with someone else, disappeared with a sealing thud. But Jack's feet slid off the side of the examination table and hit the floor hard. The rest of him followed from the long pad and now Jack was standing, swaying like a rotating top. He disappeared, too.

The hallway was the same, but he noticed more about it now, like how it wasn't all one color. It was grey, but it also had splotches of white and black and even a big red spot once, over in a corner. The corners where the wall met the floor were no longer orthodox, but steady slopes that collected garbage nothing like corners do. Ingenious.

As far as Jack could see, there weren't any doors, so he pounded his way forward with his heavy, dumb feet. He came to a Y in the road and took a left. There was no one around.

# # #

Jack turned a corner and damn if there weren't trees down there—a lot of very tall trees in a back yard, replacing the hallway and its slippery, smooth floor. He stopped in the yard and took deep breaths of night air, stared toward the night sky and the leafless tops of the trees. Jack felt like he was one of them, planted numbly into the ground.

There was a house, too, and he made his way to a tree

ODOM

near the back, notched a toe and took hold of the trustworthiest branch. His muscles contracted and burned, and Jack was into the air and up against the bark of the tree. He forced himself to his knees and then grasped for the next branch ahead, again and again until he was as far as he needed to be.

He began to work his knees to the side, sliding himself along the bark of the final branch, toward the window ledge and to the bricks of the house. With his breath hanging as clouds before his lips, Jack braced himself with another branch that grew truly diagonal until he was able to reach the window and open it with his smudged hands. He took hold of the gritty, sandy, brick window sill and pulled himself into the opening. With an extra thrust, he pulled his legs through and fell to the floor of the room with a thud. He was sweating and wet.

It took awhile for things to develop clearly, for things to become tangible. But as this happened, the fog around Jack lifted and a terrible lump in his thirsty throat swelled like a clinched fist.

He couldn't stand near her at first, but she was there, right there—with her hair brushed down over her shoulders, black and streaked with strands of brown, her skin blending into it all. The neckline of white cloth was in tight contrast across her neck. She looked pleasant.

But none of that helped very much. It was no consolation. It didn't hide anything, the fact that she looked peaceful and beautiful and young and pleasant. There was certainly nothing pleasant about it. All the good things one could say about her just made it seem all the more horrible.

He paced about and examined the bedding around her. From a distance Jack could see the flowers and all the white in there with her, all the white, but he couldn't bring himself to move any closer to her. He knew it was a bad idea. He knew it would

MINUS 55

not bring about any feeling that would make him better—no solace, no asylum. He believed he should stay back. He should keep a distance.

The pacing stopped and Jack knelt down to the floor—where he couldn't see her any longer—and he tried to cry. He tried again and again to let a little out. He really thought he should be able to let go, but there was nothing coming. It was trapped inside him—all jammed up.

When he got up to walk away, back to the window, he stopped for awhile and waited. He took a lot of deep breaths and waited for the emotions to come. He wanted something to happen. He waited for something to happen. When he turned back around, the door to Sarah's room flew open and the technicians rushed toward him. Technician number two jammed something into Jack's leg and it tightened up with pain.

"Motherfucker!" Jack slurred pathetically and angrily — spit spraying from his mouth as he yelled. "Motherfuckers!"

Then he went to the ground. Technician number two backed away with the needle in his hand. He went back to tech number one who was standing over Sarah, his arm resting at the corner of her wooden box.

As Jack melted into the cold, hard floor, he could hear one of the technicians say to Sarah, "He coulda got us fired right outta here." Then the men laughed.

Sarah said nothing.

# # #

Everything came into focus again, back in Jack's room—stopped spinning around and pounding. He had a new wound to add to the left-side collection—a nice wrap of gauze around his upper bicep. It had a deep red spot in the middle that struggled through several layers of surgical white. It looked like the Japanese flag and stung like hell when he looked at it.

ODOM

Thoughts were starting to come back, but everything was confused and fuzzy. The bloody spot on his arm didn't quite match up with his recollection of trees. Jack realized that some strange time had passed while he wasn't paying any attention. But what did it matter?

There was no longer a pitcher of water on the table next to the bed. One of the cups was still there, but it was dry as bones, as dry as Jack's mouth. He looked to the corner for his box of personals, but all of that was gone, too. Just the underwear remained, balled up on the floor next to the door.

He thought about getting up, but nothing would move. His legs felt like they had heavy, steel rods running through them, pinning him to the bed. He got a finger going so he could scratch the stubble in the fold between his neck and head, and his whole arm came alive. It searched the breast pocket in his T-shirt for cigarettes, but came away disappointed. It looked into the cup again for the smallest droplet of water, disappointed. It went back to sleep and Jack closed his eyes. He shut down.

# # #

Lyle was there, sitting at the foot of the bed in one of the metal chairs. His forearms were braced on his legs, holding the rest of him up. For awhile after Jack realized he was there, he entertained a fantasy that Lyle had come to put an end to the whole charade.

"Sorry, Jack. We got everything straightened out with that whole mix up in the spiral chain of technology. We don't need you anymore, Jack. We're really sorry about this and all," Lyle would say. "I'm almost embarrassed to have to do this."

He and Jack would then smoke a couple of cigarettes, have a couple laughs. And then it would all be over, lights out by way of a merciful bullet through a grateful brain.

Jack opened his eyes.

126

MINUS 55

"Rise and shine," Lyle said.

# # #

"I'm thirsty."

"Yeah?"

"Uh–huh."

Lyle nodded. "Hmmm," he said. "You want me to get some water for you or something—a little water?"

Jack nodded his chin into his chest. He still wasn't moving much. That one hand was back, but not much else. Lyle wasn't moving much, either. He certainly wasn't getting Jack any water.

"Alright," Lyle said. "So...uh...how's everything going? How ya feeling?"

Jack shrugged as best he could. "I'm a little thirsty."

Lyle nodded and considered it with his eyebrows. He fumbled with the inside pocket of his jacket, where he usually kept his cigarettes, but his cigarettes were now sitting on his partner's desk. He had been instructed not to give Jack any water or smokes and was now questioning why he had even come back into the room.

"Can I ask a question?" Jack asked.

"Sure, Jack," Lyle answered. "Of course you can ask a question."

Jack pushed himself up the bed toward the headboard the best he could, but it only made him more uncomfortable. His head was at a bad angle. Lyle went over to him and adjusted his pillow a bit, trying to help, and Jack got to his question.

"Can I get some water?" he asked and rubbed at his eyes with his swollen fingertips. They were throbbing and irritated his eyes like they had something foreign on them. His eyes began watering.

"I tell you what," Lyle said. "I'll go see if I can get some for you."

Lyle waited for Jack to respond, but he didn't. His eyes just watered. And then he went for the water.

Jack grabbed the cup off the table and held it in his lap. He was thirsty and sore, and the spot on his arm was still growing.

# # #

Jack waited as the red spot stopped its progress toward the edges of the white wrap, stopped growing a deeper red. He'd put the cup down, knocked it off the table and onto the floor where it spun around and stopped uncomfortably. For a moment he'd considered getting out of bed to set the cup right again, but his legs still weren't cooperating, so he just chose to stop looking at it. It was real, real quiet. No air conditioning had kicked in and nobody had stopped by the room to look in on him or say, "Hello." Jack figured maybe a half hour had passed. Or maybe it had been days.

Lyle came in. "Still awake?" he said. He looked more comfortable. He put one hand on the chair at the foot of the bed. The other stayed in his pocket. "Oh wait. Hold on." He walked out again, briskly. Jack waited awhile longer.

When Lyle came back for the second time, he had the water—another little cup that was half–empty.

"I need you to take this," he said and pulled from his pocket another one of the horse pills that the technicians had wielded. It was another red one.

Without question, Jack took the pill and swallowed it down. Then he took the water. He swished it around in his mouth, irrigating everything. Then he pushed the pill the rest of the way down his throat where it could go about its business of rendering him most certainly unconscious. He was getting to like the idea of sleep. His subconscious had far more promise and was far

MINUS 55

more interesting to him than his conscious, although he couldn't remember the specifics of it. The way he saw it, he was all fucked up when he was awake—and just plain fucked. When he was asleep, he was just asleep.

Lyle, who smelled of fresh cigarettes, sat down in the chair next to the bed. Jack flicked the little cup that had contained the water onto the floor and let out a little belch that did more harm than good.

"Water good?" Lyle asked.

Jack nodded. He didn't feel it would be worth the effort to ask for more, so he assumed a position of contentment and let the conversation die an impotent death.

After a few minutes, Lyle left.

ODOM

"Lights Out"

There was a little peace. Jack shut his eyes to block out the broken, kaleidoscopic visions he couldn't blink his way out of. His eyeballs seemed to be floating freely in some thick liquid, moving about without control. It made him sick to his stomach again.

There was silence, absolute, not even the occasional ruffle of bed clothes or the scratch of an unshaved face. Everything had gone numb, gone the way of the legs with the steel rods in them, and Jack made no attempt to remedy that. There was breathing and that was about it.

A song, however, played in Jack's head. It was nothing in particular, just fragments of this song and that, strung together with transitional phrases. He wrote some of those transitions on his own, right there on the spot, and it filled what little of him was left with pride. It was all really nice, very impressive, and the piece grew more and more grand at every turn. There were soft and subtle moments and moments of musical rage slamming against the interior walls of his skull.

At the end of the song, just before another was set to begin, the door opened. Jack thought about opening his eyes but found himself insufficiently motivated. It was just too goddamn much.

# # #

There were lots of them but only certain ones talked. Jack wondered about Lyle and Armand, if they were there. He couldn't hear them. There was one guy to the left, where a chair had been, who talked more than everybody else. He seemed to be leading the tour. He said things like, "Gentlemen, here he is—the man of the hour," or something to that effect. Jack liked him very much. He seemed very professional, a real showman. But he was neither Lyle nor Armand.

Jack also heard him use the words "sir" and "sirs." Figured from a bed, full of drugs, and eyes closed—there were about seven "sirs," and that included the guy doing most of the talking.

The visit contained entirely long moments of silence, broken up with short bursts of monotonous soliloquy. There was some muffled coughing—into hands, presumably. Jack pictured seven men in green military outfits holding their hats in front of their dicks and rocking back and forth on their heels, standing in a semi-circle around his bed. He had them smiling.

It was almost sleep time and Jack stayed perfectly still, felt he had to. The body part of him had already succumbed to whatever was wicked inside the most recent pill. He didn't feel anything but his head anymore. It was as if it had come away from the neck and was being held tight in a soft, velvet vice. All he could feel was his head and face not moving.

"Gentle*men*," said the man on the left, and Jack heard the shuffle and turn of well-shod feet toward the door. One by one, single file from the room and down the hall, they left the same way they had come in—with a "gentlemen."

# # #

Jack was barely around for the arrival of the next group, kept sinking deeper into the bed. He didn't see them but they seemed to bring the cold when they came—cold people dressed in white and working like termites. That's what they seemed like—termites. There was no talking, just a low moan thrown out occasionally with none of it thrown toward Jack. He started

ODOM

another song—started it small and simple, worked with it delicately—and it took him through, for a very long time, to nothing but the black.

"The Bionic Hand"

The sounds of other people in the room—the termites—were starting to filter back into Jack's ears. They echoed like underwater noise off the big light fixtures that hung stiff and mechanical over him, over his bed. From somewhere, it had been a long way back. He still couldn't open his eyes.

He was strapped down again, his legs at the ankles and his arms at the wrists. Jack's left arm also had a strap around the upper part, tight around the bicep, that gripped him when the muscle flexed. His breathing was strained—like he needed to yawn, but couldn't. His whole chest seemed to hum with heartburn—focused at a center point just left of his sternum and flaring out in a web pattern. It was tingling, making a buzzing between his ears.

Jack wondered where he was as the voices came in stronger, although no more clearly. He knew he wasn't in his room anymore. The bed was different. It was harder, less comfortable. And there was too much going on—too much activity for his room. His room had been a place to pass the time, to wait, a lobby of slow sedation. And he wasn't waiting anymore. Things had become busy around him.

The lights were bright and hot on Jack's face and he could make out their yellow–white glow behind his eyelids. He was too frightened to open his eyes—scared of being blinded, although he reasoned that the men doing all the chattering around him would never do anything to blind him. He was important. They knew that. That's why they were behind those big light fixtures, doing

ODOM

their work and making the room busy. Because he was an important man.

As Jack weighed his own importance, someone grabbed his left hand and there was a sharp, piercing prick of a needle sliding into the top of it just above the fingers. Teeth gnashed. There was pressure as the liquid entered, a throbbing as the hand was filling up.

And then there was nothing. The hand was gone, slowly up to the elbow where the cessation of feeling halted.

Jack felt he should go back to sleep, go back to the black, but he was stuck between sleepy shade and the yellow–white lights of his new room.

# # #

The lights pulled back and Jack opened his eyes just enough to see through his eyelashes, just enough to adjust. Everything was white, turning baby blue. There were men, dressed in white from head to toe, turning baby blue, motionless and watching, waiting. They stood around waiting for the card trick, the punch line. Some of them had little smiles on their faces—pale to watery red as everything was coming back into focus. All of them looked the same, like they'd just popped out of a mold and put their uniforms on.

Jack took a deep breath and the burning in his chest changed over to a tightness with an occasional jolt or electric twinge. He raised his head off the pillow and one of the men came to him.

"Take it easy," he said and he put his hand behind Jack's head, lowered it gently back to the pillow. He had a soft, motherly voice. "Just relax awhile longer. No hurry, no hurry," soft-talking, buying more time to stand around and marvel, more time for he and his baby–blue associates.

As Jack's head hit the pillow, there was movement around

MINUS 55

him—some of the men moved. Others stood admiring. There was another twinge in his chest and then some murmuring from the men, another twinge and some murmuring. As the twinges grew more frequent, the murmuring got more concentrated and the baby blue men approached Jack's slab and leaned over him. He looked up at them expecting to meet their eyes with his, but there were none for him. All eyes were away, down to the left, down his left side to the numbness that started at his elbow and ended just beyond the fingertips.

   Jack followed their eyes with his own, but could see nothing but a blue veil obscuring all of him from his left elbow beyond.

ODOM

"New Reality"

Everybody was gone but those damn lights were still there, right in Jack's face. The door was slowly shutting, pulling the curtain on the baby blue medicine gang, and Jack flexed his left hand, or at least he thought he did. There was that blue veil blocking a visual confirmation, but he imagined himself closing his fingers into a fist and then flaring them back out—over and again to send a message of normalcy to his unconvinced brain.

He held up his right hand like he was displaying a watch or dinner bracelet for sale. It stood at attention like five dancers, all five fingers paused in the air above his wrist, which was bent against the tightness of a nylon strap. He clentched a fist. Over and again, he was clenching and unclenching—right hand in the open, left hand in his mind. It was damn–easy entertainment, but enough to occupy his slow decay, soaking in all those drugs and all that situation.

The straps at his ankles were becoming more uncomfortable every second he pondered them. The legs had come alive again. A real trade off—strapped down legs for a nonexistent hand. It was the deal that had Jack thirsting for nothing more than comfort. All he wanted in the world was to bend at the knees.

He had already decided, just after he woke up, that the quicker the whole debacle ended, the better everything would be. While he was under sedation, he was happy, or at least not unhappy. He was unaware, disengaged. There was nothing while

MINUS 55

he was asleep, not even black. What was black? he thought. Everything didn't turn to black, it turned to nothing. And black is not nothing. Black is black.

Jack burned upstairs, above the eyebrows. There was a fire on up there. He was alone in his deep thinking, thinking nothing.

# # #

Bill came in, or at least that's what his name badge read. He came in, whoever he was—Bill or someone successfully impersonating a Bill. He came in and sat down.

"Is your name Bill?" Jack asked slowly, laughed like he was drunk.

Bill looked down at the tag and back at Jack. He opened his eyes real wide and no expression came to his face. "That's what they tell me." Then he smiled.

Bill wasn't baby blue. He was off–white and fuzzy around edges, seemed to use the light of the room to intensify himself. He sat a tray down on the floor in front of his feet, next to Jack's bed, off to the right side and under that hand of Jack's which had only recently stopped dancing.

"So, you're Jack."

Jack nodded. "Bill?"

Bill nodded.

"You, Bill. Me, Jack." Jack wondered why they weren't sending Bill to his death.

"I'm here to shave you," Bill said.

"Save me?"

"No, *shave*. To *shave* you."

Jack closed his eyes and popped his shoulders by straining them against the straps. "My face?"

Bill gathered the tray and put it on the side of the bed. "Yes," he answered. "For pictures."

ODOM

Jack nodded. "I gotta take pictures."

"We've got people to take the pictures," Bill said. He was spreading a lather in his hands, concentrating. "All you have to do is look good when they start taking them." He leaned in with the lather and Jack pressed his head into the pillow as far as he could.

"Relax, now. I have done this before," Bill said.

Jack settled and the lather went onto the cheeks, then down under the chin and onto the neck a little. Bill stopped for a second and pushed the two bright lights out of Jack's face with the back of his hand. It was better then. Everything was taken down a notch.

"You the barber?"

Bill laughed. "No. Just do it sometimes. When they need it done." He got the chin real good and started the upper lip. He was careful, careful not to get any into Jack's nose and mouth. "Actually," Bill continued, "most folks don't make it this far—to the shavin' stage, you see."

Jack said, "Huh?", but the lather kept going on.

The job finished, Bill wiped his hands on a white towel that hung from his waist. He leaned back in and made some adjustments with his fingertips, then wiped those off on the towel, too.

"Just sit still for awhile," Bill said. He looked at his watch. It was like Armand's. Then he leaned back in his chair with his hands in his lap.

"You think you can do me a favor?" Jack asked.

Bill moved nary a muscle.

"Undo the straps—the leg straps?" Jack asked.

Bill looked down at the legs and then he looked down at the side of the bed, down toward his own feet. He reached down and grabbed another strap—one that looked like a weightlifting belt—and he tossed it across Jack's waist. Around the other side was another strap and Bill connected the two and pulled them snug across Jack's hips. Then he undid the feet straps. It was the kind of deal Jack had been looking for.

"Thanks," he said and he raised his legs slowly off the bed, pointed the bottoms of his feet toward the ceiling. Holding his hips firm and tightening the muscles in his stomach, he let the feet fall free, heels toward his ass, like imminently doomed pendulums. His knees popped and cracked like hot popcorn and Jack let out a groan of anti–pleasure. "Goddamn," he said breathlessly. "That feels good." He breathed at a post orgasmic gait and worked the legs some more.

He'd worked it down from four straps to three. Just like an act of magic. "Do you know what I do for a living?" Jack asked Bill, who was back to his statuesque posture next to the bed.

"No," Bill said.

# # #

Alone again, Jack felt like a funeral attraction. People showed up to look at him, get a last good look. No one talked to him, just around. He longed to roll over onto his side. He would have preferred to have been strapped in belly–down with his left arm sticking off the other side. He believed his head would have felt better that way, more together. But instead, he was flat on his back with his arms spread out like wings—like he was in mid back–dive.

Lyle came in. "Jesus fuckin' Chr*ist!*" he said. He shook his head as the door swung closed behind him. He was packing a cigarette on the back of a pack.

"Undo this strap over here," Jack said. "Undo the right one." He was slow–talking, sedate, and had the appearance of being happy.

ODOM

"The *right* one?"

Jack tugged violently on the right strap, bounced his right arm against the bed. It made him tired, made his heart pound in his wide open, vibrating chest.

"You're not gonna do anything crazy..." said Lyle.

"Whadda ya mean, crazy?" Jack said in between breaths.

"Don't get anywhere close to that left arm," Lyle said. "Stay away from that arm. You go for that arm, Jack, and I'm gonna shoot ya. 'He escaped and came for me with that right arm.' That's what I'll tell them." Lyle took off the strap.

Jack shook out the arm, wound his wrist around in ovals. He made little ovals with his shoulder. His ass itched and he worked his way onto the bare skin, past the sheet and medical pants, and scratched the hell out of it. It felt about as good as things can feel. It made his heart race.

Lyle had his cigarette in his mouth, but it wasn't going. It was just dangling. After Jack had chased away every itch and tickle on his right hemisphere, he noticed the cigarette again. He exhaled a long breath. He could barely catch enough air in his lungs to keep him going. He had to lay still for awhile. "Hey, man," still catching his breath. "You gonna... give... me one a those."

"I figured you might need one," Lyle said, and he fumbled in his shirt pocket for his pack of smokes. "That's one of the reasons I stopped by, actually. I'm pretty smart sometimes, you know what I mean. I've got a little bit of insight into things. I knew you'd be needin' a smoke...that you deserved to have one and all, so I stopped by a little early. Last wishes sort of thing."

Lyle got Jack started on his cigarette and pulled an ashtray out of his pocket. He pointed to his temple a few times and smiled, winked. Jack took short drags off the cigarette and blew them out on the next quick breath. It was difficult for him to

140

smoke while lying flat on his back. Occasionally, an ash would fall down onto his face, where the beard had been, but it would just slide down along the cheeks to the bed clothes. His face was a smooth face.

That Bill had done some kinda job.

# # #

Next cigarette.

"What's next?" Jack asked.

"Ah," said Lyle, took a drag. Exhaled and smiled, nodded his head. "Next. Next is getting ready for the big show." He turned toward the bed and toward Jack, became very serious—much more earnest than usual. "We've got to follow through on this thing, Jack—make everything final, set everything right again, you know."

"Soon?"

"Ah, yes. Very soon." Lyle was nodding and smiling as he took a drag from his smoke.

It was almost show–time and Jack got the feeling in his guts that he always got when show–time was fast approaching. He sucked in some of his cigarette and looked away from Lyle, up toward the ceiling. He got an uneasy feeling in his stomach and throat, and took the deepest breaths possible in order to make everything better. He wanted everything to be better. Wanted to be off that bed, out of that room. Wanted to breathe real air again.

As they waited, Lyle got another cigarette going. The room was quickly filling with grey like it was being pushed in through tubes behind the vents in the ceiling. It was no longer medical.

# # #

More guys came into the room, two more. They were in white and they carried clothing with them. They didn't say a word at first, just came in quickly, let the door swing shut behind

ODOM

them, and sat a helmet on the end of Jack's bed. They hung a one-piece, baby-blue suit of clothes on a free-standing apparatus that looked to have been made just for that purpose. Each nodded to Jack and then to Lyle, smiled the same smile. And then they addressed Agent Gardetto. "We're gonna give him a little shot and then get him dressed."

Lyle nodded.

Jack wondered why they were talking to Lyle and not him, and why they were talking so softly. Lyle wasn't getting any shot. He wasn't getting blasted off into the great void. There were ideas lining up in the tunnels in Jack's brain, ideas locking together like puzzle pieces from an assortment of dissimilar puzzles. There were things going on that Jack couldn't figure. All of these men, like a family of men, living under the ground, kidnapping people from the overworld and doing experiments on them under the guise of "Hey, listen man, we're just trying to save the world." It was like an evil, homosexual army—a big spider queen birthing them from the top of the pyramid.

Suddenly, Jack had rebellious thoughts. He fantasized about running wild and free through the labrynthian halls and murdering the entirety of the underground virus. He looked at Lyle and Lyle smiled and smoked a cigarette. Lyle always smiled and smoked a cigarette.

When Jack turned back to the two men at the foot of the bed, they had moved. One of them was bending toward his left arm, a long needle extending from his hand. Above the curtain that blocked off the elbow and beyond, Jack could see him slowly plunging the syringe, releasing liquid into his bloodstream. But there was no feeling, no sensation of the needle going in or the liquid. None that wasn't trumped up by his brain, which was soaking in all those drugs and all that situation.

The other man, the counterpart, was coming up on Jack's

MINUS 55

right side. He was moving like a parade balloon, bouncing, being held aloft by invisible ropes held by invisible hands. He was carrying a big, red, white, and blue helmet, and he was smiling.

# # #

The phantom pain in the left arm faded as the left-side guy returned to the front of the bed. Not thinking, Jack tried to retrieve his arm from beyond the curtain and jolted himself enough to realize that his head was starting to swim, the room was becoming slowly unhinged.

He settled back against the pillow. "Fuck," he said, but nobody heard him. The helmet was next to him, hovering patiently. He took a few good breaths and cleared his throat.

"Let's get this helmet on you, Jack," Helmet said.

It was red, white and blue, and looked serious. Jack pulled his head off the pillow to allow the helmet to slide on. He felt like he had already escaped gravity, like he was free-floating against the straps that remained in place. It was his new reality.

Next, they stood him up—took the straps from his waist and hips and helped him to his feet. Lyle stayed out of the way. He'd put his last cigarette out and he was keeping a close eye, an inspectful eye, on the action. The time for his last task had also come. Get Jack to the launch site on time; have him looking good for the camera.

Before Jack ever thought to sneak a look at it, his left hand was gloved and again out of site. The restriction imposed by the helmet was sufficient in dissuading him from looking around too much. He looked straight forward through the narrow opening. Peripherally, he could see the sides of the opening, as well as above and below. It reminded him of the old underwater science fiction movies. A guy floating around in the deep, mostly naked, a big helmet over his head with a grill on the front. He could hear the water going by.

ODOM

He bent at the waist and neck as best he could and saw that he had become completely suited. Now, *he* was baby blue—the color of a corpse. The suit was tight like another skin. It felt good, his new reality.

Lyle came into the picture, entering stage right on Jack's screen, and he smiled into the helmet. Jack smiled back—a real plaque and tar contest.

"We can take the helmet off, now, I think," Gardetto said and he looked to the two tailors. They nodded back, stage left.

Lyle unlatched the right side and one of the others did the left. The air came back. Lyle smiled again.

"Feeling good?" he asked.

Jack nodded. He was hovering between contentment and acquiescence. It was an extremely tolerable existence, like liberation. Like a kid has freedom—not to do anything they want, but rather the freedom to not do anything. Jack was calm, breathing easily and not doing anything.

He stepped onto the conveyer belt which had just materialized at his feet and he went out the door and into the hallway. He was preceded by Lyle and followed by the other two gentlemen who had just seen him naked with a red, white, and blue helmet on.

# # #

The hall scrolled steadily by, the walls on Jack's right and left, and then, the belt they were on—Jack, Lyle, and the tailors—took a hard left down an endless hallway. Jack looked over his shoulder and saw the tailors. One of them carried his helmet. The other stood motionless with his arms down to his side. They were looking past him.

In front of Jack and a little below him, Lyle checked his watch, then checked it again. He looked over his shoulder and gave Jack a reaffirming nod, a smile.

MINUS 55

Jack felt like there was only the suit holding him up, like he was being relieved of his humanity—artificial strength being pumped in through some hidden plumbing. Up ahead, far down the hall, he could see a splash of light—below them on the decline—a light from which the overhead lights seemed to be emerging. It gave the illusion that *they* were standing still and everything around them was moving. He had to look down, past the wide, hooped neck of the suit, to break the illusion.

The light ahead began to open up, grow larger, as they were pulled toward it. It bent the shadows on the floor that lay ahead, made them concave with blinding yellow light. Jack turned around again and looked past the tailors. There was a light back there, too, a dull light, back from where they had come. They were half–way home.

As they reached the end of the belt, the bottom of their long descent, the yellow light blossomed, opened up into the bright outside. The sun was high on the horizon, right in front of them. Jack tried to shield his eyes from it, but found his hands too heavy. He couldn't see a thing. He tried to focus on the ground, but all he saw was yellow—yellow spots and blotches, perfect circles moving around like lively bacteria. He tried to blink his way out of it, got his eyes watering by yawning. When he came around, there were a lot of feet around him—more than eight. There were his own, there were Lyle's, and then there were some off to the side, off to either side, lined up side by side.

Jack looked up and there were many men in front of him, forming a hallway with walls of rigid bodies. They laid out a path to the pad, standing erect as the structure they were leading him to. He averted his eyes from the glass spacecraft as soon as he saw it lying there on its side. The sun was shooting light through it, covering Jack in a hot, colorful bath.

Transparent spacecraft, Jack thought. Transparent space-

ODOM

craft.

There was a man down at the base of the rocket, filling it up with fuel that looked like dirty lemonade. Hand–pumpin' it. He appeared to be smeared with grease, wearing a service station outfit, and had a chewed–up toothpick in his mouth. He waved to Jack and smiled, pulled a red handkerchief out of his back pocket and wiped his brow, said "Whew!" Then he nodded to Lyle and went back to the fueling.

"Follow me, Jack," said Lyle. They were moving, moving past the men in green, in blue, in white. The men didn't move or look directly at Jack. They looked on past each other, into the endless, brown grass.

As they moved between the lines, Jack felt cool air stinging his cheeks through the refracting light, getting down into the bowl that surrounded the base of his neck like a bottomless saucer for a coffee cup. The rest of his body felt warm—stiff and warm.

As Jack looked back, the men in line were turning to watch as he passed them by. It was all set up—a tight plan, a good layout of what to do. When Jack turned back around, he and Lyle were at the base of the launch site and the base of the rocket. It was massive, like the plastic wrapper of a New York skyscraper lying on its side—rigid, filled with a million exploding fireflies.

The tailors reappeared, emerged from the ship's glow, and stepped forward to attach Jack's helmet to the rest of the suit. With a click it swiveled into place. Through the red–tinted front shield Jack could see the men checking things, orbiting him like little white satellites, connecting him to his suit, starting the symbiosis. He could see their lips move as they talked to one another, but he couldn't hear what they were saying. Lyle looked down at the tailors as they slowly circled, his lips moving, too, but Jack could hear nothing but a hum that ran up through him, amplified in his head.

Lyle looked up from the tailors and into Jack's face. "Can you hear me, Jack?" he asked.

Jack didn't respond. He understood the question by reading Lyle's lips, but he didn't respond. He felt embarrassed, like he was being singled out. Is he talking to me?—he thought.

"He can't hear me," Lyle said, smirked, and shook his head. He was looking down at the satellites again. Jack's body wanted to sweat, but it couldn't. His face felt flushed. After a few seconds, he could now hear the tailor's working on him. He heard everything with clarity.

When Lyle looked up again, a screech tore through Jack's body so thoroughly, so harsh and shrill that he could feel his whole body convulse and shiver, kept collected only by the exoskeletal suit.

"Whoa, whoa, whoa!" Lyle said, seeing the pained expression on Jack's face, and got down on the tailor's level. Things jumped back to normal, although there remained a loud ringing in Jack's ears. It was painful——major car damage, Jack figured—and something he would never have to worry about. Nary a doctor's visit.

# # #

"Can you hear me?" Lyle asked Jack.

Jack nodded inside the helmet. He could hear himself breathing.

Lyle smiled at him and put his arm on Jack's shoulder. The tailor's stepped back. "Okay, Jack. Are you ready?"

Jack looked down the side of the rocket. The glass panes were riveted and stitched together with ribs of metal, and the sunlight danced around inside the payload like jackpot lights. On the side in enormous blue letters and red numbers was written: "Ea–0055." There was a massive structure built up around the

ODOM

base, sitting on the pad like the skeleton of a hollow building. It was to hold the rocket in place for its launch. It was the framework for the final stage.

    Lyle turned Jack and walked him over to the platform next to the rocket. There was a loud ringing in his ears and the suit continued to make noise. Jack could also hear the outside wind blowing. Somehow he heard this. A speaker system. Something. He wasn't exactly sure.

    Lyle turned Jack around and put him on the platform, facing outward toward the colorful assembly. The lines of men were looking toward him, extending all the way back to the emergence of the underground tunnel. The two tailors had taken their places in the closer of the two lines.

    Again, Lyle turned Jack, faced him toward the rocket this time. Jack looked up as high as he could, but still couldn't see where the side of the rocket rounded to the top. It had to be six stories off the ground lying on its side, he imagined. A phone booth for god, filling steadily with transparent fuel.

    Lyle got Jack's attention and asked again if he was ready. Jack nodded. Lyle pushed a button on the platform floor with the toe of his shoe and a railing came up around the two men. When the rail was up to about four feet, the platform began to rise steadily alongside the shimmering skin. Jack shivered as a flutter filled his stomach and a chill slid down his back. They were climbing above the audience behind them. Jack didn't want to turn around, didn't want to move for fear of falling, so he imagined the scene— all men saluting, feeling prideful and hopeful about the future of mankind and their place in it, and then scrambling for cover as the rocket heated up and fired.

    As the rocket cornered and started to curve the other way, Jack looked up again, could see the sun hanging in the wide open sky above the glass rectangle. They were more then half-way up. The red-tinted shield in front of his face allowed him to stare directly into the burning ball, let the perfect symmetry burn onto his eyeballs—a perfect circle shooting energy into the unfillable universe.

Once they reached a certain height, Jack could make out figures on top of the colossus, one of them moving about while the others kept still, blending into one another. It was as if they were standing on the air, levitating high above everything. As they got closer, Jack could see that the one in motion was Armand. He was paying attention to the details.

"There's Agent Locke," Lyle said.

"Yes, there he is," Jack said to himself, although he couldn't hear it.

The platform was nearly to the top and Jack got another series of sensations from his stomach and spine. When the platform became one with the floor on which Armand and the three others were standing, it clicked into place and relaxed. The front gate slid down through the floor and Lyle hopped off. He reached back for Jack, grabbed him by the elbow of his suit and walked him toward the others. Now *he* was walking on the air.

"Hello, Jack," Armand said. "Everything's running smoothly." His hair was blowing a little in the wind, thickets of hair flipping back and forth like irregular windshield wipers across his forehead. He spoke louder than usual, over the wind. "Everything's real good," he said.

Jack nodded toward his faceplate. Everything's real good.

Lyle left Jack alone, standing just off the platform which awaited anyone who required a return to the ground, and he and Armand discussed the final details. They knelt down beside a chair that faced them, its back rising above the nose-cone of the ship. It looked like a nightmare barber's chair, an electric chair. There was a lot of wiring behind it. Jack thought it looked a

ODOM

mess, like something in horrible disorder, but no one else seemed concerned with what it looked like. Beneath it was the only solid part of the ship, a black rectangle.

A man crawled out of the hole behind the chair, out of a chamber in the rocket—pulled himself up and joined three others on the rostrum. They talked among themselves, but frugally. Two of the gentlemen, including the one recently birthed from the rocket's innards, were dressed in blue, one was in white and the other was in green. They stood in a line, according to color, like a baseball team lines up along the chalk for the national anthem, only leaning forward to engage in conversation that Jack couldn't make out.

Lyle and Armand went to the line and talked to each man. There were smiles and handshakes, a couple slaps on shoulders. Then Lyle and Armand returned to Jack.

"Here we go, Jack."

More sensations from Stomach and Spine.

Lyle took the right arm and Armand had the left. They led Jack to the chair. He took his seat, settled in and rested his arms on the rests and his feet on the two places for them that Armand had pointed out. It was quickly comfortable. He was more comfortable sitting down, getting a little support

in his contest with gravity.

The shoulder straps were padded metal or hard rubber, something rigid and snug, and they fell down around him like a rollercoaster mechanism. After they were in place, Lyle and Armand, along with one blue, one white, and one green man, approached Jack and his augmentations. The remaining man, the remaining blue, began to shoot pictures—several moments from every angle. He never stopped shooting, never took the silver box away from his eye.

As Lyle moved closer, he blocked out the sun that hung in

the sky on Jack's right side. The five men stood around him in a semi-circle. They were checking everything—pulling leg restraints around Jack's thighs and over his ankles, and bands for the wrists. Lyle checked the shoulder apparatus from his side and Armand got the other. The sun popped in and around Lyle's head as he worked and Jack tried to enjoy as much of it as he could. It was tough, though. He almost wished it would just go ahead and go away, tuck itself behind some clouds for awhile, stop trying to cheer him up. But it blasted away, lighting the faceplate like the red glow of dying neon.

After some tugging and jostling about—tightening the loose ends—each man took turns stepping away from the chair. The camera man changed angles, more toward the platform that had brought Jack and Lyle to the top, and he kept shooting. Jack looked from one face to the other, seeing the same expression. Hope or charity or empathy was the main theme that came across in the eyes—a generic combination of these things. And all lit up with the dancing lights.

Lyle looked to Armand and Armand stepped forward. He knelt down in front of Jack and spoke loudly, to the point of yelling.

"OK, Jack. We're about to turn you around and put you inside this baby," he said. "You read me?"

Jack nodded, thought yes.

"Alright. Then we're going to stand this baby upright," Armand said and he illustrated with his arm, "and get everything underway. We're very excited, Jack," he said. He looked to his right, at the camera man, and then back to Jack. He smiled and the wind hooked some more hair across his forehead. "We're all very excited. You excited?" He raised his voice even louder.

Jack nodded, thought yes, very excited.

# # #

ODOM

Jack was locked in—restraints across the ankles, the thighs, the wrists, and a harness over the shoulders—locked in tight. And so he was, for the most part, finished—in seemingly more ways than just one. He looked out across the landscape. As far left as he could see, all the suit and the restraints would allow, stood the building of trees, one corner of it at least. They were a good distance away from it now. In all other directions was horizon, all lit up with sunlight.

Jack looked through the line–up of men who stood in front of him, stood with the wind pounding at them. They were talking, going over things that were written down on official papers. He looked past them, down the length of the rocket to the base where the launch scaffolding was. It was a skyscraper, up with the clouds. He had seen buildings being built, the frameworks showing without the meat and skin, and it looked like this. As he looked toward the top, he thought of Paris, and he felt as if the whole apparatus was swaying with the wind.

Slowly and mechanically, Jack's chair raised off the stage and stopped two feet above it. He sat poised in the air, eye level with everyone in front of him. There was more discussion about what was on the official papers, a huddle, and Jack imagined the conversation: "What do we do next?" "Push that one." "No, no, no. Don't push *that* one."

The whole idea of men standing on top of a rocket, preparing to launch him to his death, on some level, filled Jack with satisfaction. A sedate smile struggled to his lips and his eyebrows raised up off his eyes for a moment—as long as he could sustain it.

What the crew was actually talking about was whether or not they should hook up the hand while they were down there or wait until they had Jack and the rocket standing upright.

# # #

MINUS 55

The chair started backward and the six men in front of Jack, cameraman off to the side, followed him as he moved closer to the head of the rocket, toward his cockpit hole. It was like a ride, the most thrilling one in the park, and Jack had been selected to give it the first test run.

The men were obviously excited by the prospects before them. They were glad to be at work doing worthwhile things. It was too much for Jack, however. He wished they would turn away and stop smiling and looking content toward him so he could return to playing out their intentions and dialogue in his head. His progress backward and theirs forward only reminded him that he was dying.

The chair eased to a stop. Jack really felt big. That suit was starting to get to him. It seemed so large. He could feel the weight of it shift on his skin as the chair moved about.

As five of the men got on the platform and headed back to the ground, Armand approached Jack again—came up as close as he could.

"OK, Jack," he said. He was really shouting now. The wind was really blowing. "We're gonna send you up. It's all yours from here." He nodded his head and smiled, waved.

The heads of Lyle and the four others had disappeared and the platform reached the top again—unoccupied. Armand glanced at it as it arrived. He stood up straight, put his hands on his hips, and took in a deep breath.

"Hey, you in there? You listening, Jack?" Locke yelled, squinting. "I just wanted to say good luck." He nodded his head and raised his palm toward Jack and his chair. "And thanks."

Armand put his hands on his knees and peered in, looked into the illuminated faceplate that sat atop the motionless suit. "Just think of that pretty girl, Jack. I know you'll be with her very soon.

ODOM

"I'll see you topside, OK. I'll see you in a couple minutes. Good luck, Jack," Armand said and he got on the platform and waved.

Jack watched him through the glowing glass until he disappeared into the bottom of his visor. He was all by himself again and his seat started to move, like it was running the show autonomously. It rotated clockwise toward the front of the rocket, spinning Jack toward the sun. He could feel the heat scan across his face and his eyeballs as he stared off into the horizon, unflinchingly. Before long he was looking straight down the nose of the rocket, at the light that broke and scattered away from it. It slopped away, about twenty feet in front of him, into nothing but mile long horizon. Through the glare he couldn't actually see where it ended.

The chair began to lower. It dropped more quickly than it had gone backwards or turned, and Jack was soon below the surface, down into the black box, under the sharp shadow that cut at the surface edge above him. It was completely quiet, no wind. There was no light down there, either, only the blue sky above, reflecting weakly in one corner of the red visor.

The chair settled into the belly of the ship and the hatch above closed and Jack could hear it come together—slam shut and lock into place for several seconds. He could hear the suit again, humming several octaves lower than the ringing the tailors and Lyle had added to his ears, coming at him in harmonies. His hole was pitch black, vacuously silent, still, and Jack thought about what Armand had said before he left him to be sucked into the hole. "You'll be with her very soon. I know you'll be with her very soon. Think of that pretty girl, Jack...I know you'll be with her very soon."

Dirty tricks.

Jack had never believed in the afterlife—just as he had

MINUS 55

never believed in anything he considered to be nonsensical bullshit—but he thought about it with a new perspective now. There had been no way to supplement this kind of experience into his previous way of thinking, and so he found himself unsure about everything at once, ready to smash every belief he held. In fact, as he took in his last moments he was prepared to destroy his very belief in belief, his belief in reality. He was in a mechanical hole, strapped to a mechanical chair, a mechanical harness with the accompanying array of belts and restraining straps gripping him tightly. It wasn't real. He was a reality of one and a reality of one does not constitute any kind of reality. Things were betwixt and between to such a degree that Jack had no choice but to allow hope to emerge in the face of futility. It was either that or quitting.

Subtly, the rocket began to rise. Jack could feel a slow change in the distribution of weight on his body. It was as if he was slowly falling backward in a chair, holding a giant sack of beans in his lap. He couldn't see anything, but he could imagine the angles he had ascended to. He imagined the men on the ground, far below him now, saluting, and he pictured the gigantic scaffolding that he was approaching.

But no matter how hard he thought, and how much foundationless, directionless hope he could muster, he couldn't get one damn Sarah into his mind.

Goddamn dirty tricks.

ODOM

"Roulette"

Jack felt that he and the rocket were pretty close to ninety degrees, but he couldn't tell anything for sure anymore. As far as he was concerned, he was flat on his back. He felt like he was floating in his suit—high above the ground, floating in solid black—a starless, moonless night. He was losing his grip, becoming dead, easing in.

As his eyes struggled to collect the smallest fragment of light, the hum of the heavy suit became the sound to Jack's visions—visions of the rocket reaching its right angle, visions of the launching structure pulling him easily home. He closed his eyes and tried to breathe, took deep breaths and tried to relax. But it was difficult. He wanted to go to sleep, but he was charged. He wanted to be out of that place, but he was strapped down and locked in.

Eventually, Jack took the advice of Armand—let Sarah into the black. He had her standing in front of him. He could see her body, the way it moved or how it paused, and he had the skin just as dark and perfect as he recollected it. He remembered every adjective he'd ever used to describe her lips and eyes, but he still couldn't get it right. It wouldn't build. Her face wouldn't come in like it should.

His mind was also playing the dirty game with him. In his conscious dream he was unable to stare into her face. He wasn't able to see what she looked like. His sedately suffocating brain was turning her away and all he could see were flashes of

MINUS 55

neck and ear. He tried to put her in a context—threw some backgrounds around her. He remembered her in photographs, in the club where they'd met, in audiences, but her face was just as nondescript as everyone who was not her. And it wasn't because he didn't know, he just couldn't do it. It was defeating. He felt jettisoned.

When he looked directly at her she would disappear. If he looked to the side or above or below, he could prove to himself that she was there, but she would vanish the instant he tried to get a good look at her. The more he thought about her, the further he got from being able to make her out. She was little more than an idea with backgrounds.

As the rocket was reaching 90 degrees, the lid of the cockpit began to re–open, re–introduce Jack to the red world. When the opening was complete and the rocket sat perpendicular to the earth, there was a clang and Jack thought he could hear the wind again.

# # #

The rocket was standing next to the launch structure like a twin tower and Jack saw everything there was for him to see from the upside down position. He took a deep breath. He thought this was it. They'd reopened the cockpit just to give a last, quick look and then they were gonna shut it back up and blast that motherfucker into the great beyond, get the show on the road. This was Jack's thinking, so he took deep breaths and closed his eyes again. He found it difficult to comprehend what was going on around him and chose not to think about it in much the same fashion one chooses to stop thinking about sex with the beautiful. Not very well. He was in some kind of quasi–medical, adrenaline shock, all being mediated by some imaginary man at an imaginary terminal that controlled the physiology of the suit he was wearing. That's how he saw things.

ODOM

He was no longer curious about what was going to happen next out there in the red. He wanted that comfortable hole to close, that control panel in front of him to light up, and someone official to scream, "Yee–Hah!!!" into his ear, or something effectively that, but everything was quiet.

Instead, the chair came back to life again and began to push Jack back out into the afternoon. "Goddamn," he whispered as the sunlight reached down to him. There was a beep in his ear but nobody said anything, certainly not "yee–hah."

With a blast of sunlight, Jack's screen lit up red again and warmed the left side of his face. It blinded him for a second as his eyes re–adjusted. Felt like he was being born. He was aware of his skin again, how oily it seemed and how it tingled like there was sweat rolling from his forehead to his chin, ignoring the gravity. He squinted and tried to pull everything back into focus, but the progression from the blackness of the hole to the red afternoon caused everything to shimmer and blur. Sunlight shot down off the glass nose of the ship and bombed away at his eyes.

When he rolled his eyes back, he could see the sky and the extent of both the launch tower and the rocket. The structure for the launch was awestriking. The rocket was solid and heavy, shaped like an invisible bullet.

On both sides of the faceplate appeared men, shades of red, three on the left and three on the right. Jack looked up at them, as they also extended into his sky, and he thought about gravity again. It made his stomach turn.

# # #

Jack couldn't make out the faces of the three men on his right. They were too close to one another, looking at the one guy on the left that Jack could see. This was Armand. The two men remaining on the left were standing right in front of the sun, hovering above Jack and camouflaged in their own shadows. Armand was speaking to everyone but Jack couldn't hear what he was saying, just the hum. He could, however, see Armand's lips move and watch him use his finger to drive home the main points. It looked like he was delivering a lecture or a sermon, not an execution.

When Armand concluded his speech, the other five heads disappeared beneath Jack's vision. He could feel himself, his suit, being secured and locked down even further. When Armand pointed in the direction of Jack's left side, the action went there.

Jack considered his left side. He remembered he couldn't feel his left arm from his elbow to his fingertips. He moved the fingers on his right hand and felt them move along the inside of the suit. He sent the same message to the left side but got nothing back. Soon, the absence of feeling that ran from Jack's left fingertips to his left elbow spread to the shoulder and then out into the body cavity—slowly, like dye dispersing in water. It washed over him, over the right side and down into those fingertips. It worked down into his crotch and over his stiff knees, down into his feet and toes. His body became numb, filled up with nothing.

One of the men stood up and Jack could see half of his face in the sunlight. It spoke to Armand and made Armand's brow wrinkle and sink into his eyes, made him walk over next to it. When they again sank underneath Jack's line of sight, all that was left was the rocket, stretching into the endless sky like a brand new phallus.

As Jack waited his eyes watered. He imagined himself yawning as strong fumes began to fill his helmet. On the screen, one by one, the figures popped back up until there were six, all on the left side. They seemed focused, expectant. There was some talking, but Jack didn't even imagine what they might be saying. His eyes slammed shut and by the time he struggled

ODOM

enough to reopen them, the men were done and gone.
# # #
The fumes in Jack's head (now visible) were like bubblegum flavored morphine and he started to get more comfortable sitting there flat on his back—sitting there with the big, beautiful sky overhead, the sun shining all over him, a light refreshing breeze whipping across some water that he imagined surrounding him.

Lyle approached, waded through the red. He was upside–down and leaning over Jack from above. He gave a half–assed salute and reached into his coat to retrieve a picture, the picture of Sarah that Armand had printed out in Jack's living room. It seemed the same.

Jack could see her on the print, but not definitively, as Lyle turned the picture around to face him. He squinted against the red sky and wiped his eyes with his eyelids—pulled her in closer, the shape of her face and her black hair. As Lyle brought the picture nearer, however, she started to disappear like dye dispersing in water, reverse developing. The entire print grew blacker, bathing in a sea of red sunlight. The outline of her body and the trace of her hair dissolved as Lyle stuck the photograph to Jack's faceplate—slapped it on and rubbed his hand over it so it would stick. He then popped over to the right side of Jack's screen, from behind the black and into the red, and he smiled, again saluted. He wished Jack luck. Then he nodded and exited stage right.

Jack was in shadow. He couldn't pull the picture in at all. There was nothing to see but a black rectangle over the left eye and a red–clouded, sun–powered, sky over the right.

A few moments and the chair started retreating back inside the rocket. The red sky was closing. Jack's whole screen was turning black, from the bottom up, slowly shutting off another one of his senses.

As there was an inch or so left, Jack tried to move his head so he could take in as much of it as he could. But it was a pointless act. He wasn't even sure he could move anymore. He couldn't feel anything. And with the remaining, red inch disappearing into a half and then a quarter and an eighth, there was too little left to worry about taking any of it anyway.

Jack closed his eyes and tried to think about that girl again. The one he couldn't see. The one that was too close to his goddamn face.

# # #

Pitch black, eyes open or closed, Jack's mind turned over and again the sound of the cockpit closing, clinking together, locking shut. It was all he could hear, short of his own breathing and his own heartbeat. It wasn't that often that Jack heard the beating of his own heart, but it was always there for these situations, the situations of magnitude. The sound, the thump–thump, filled the inside of his suit and pulsated between his ears, temple to temple, like heavy–echoing electricity. It was the sound of being underwater and Jack once again felt like he was floating in his suit–floating naked and untouched between the fabric of the white costume. The sensation reminded him of his underwater escapes, each of them as part of a single, but his most recent most prevalently.

He remembered his closed eyelids becoming illuminated with red/green water—a solution of the tank water and the hot stage lights. He could feel the shackles at his wrists and ankles, neck and waist. In his mind, Jack could also hear the sound of an amplified voice. It was muddled, bouncing through the water too unintelligently to be understood, but it was there, coming in on waves like little phrases of music.

When the cockpit lights ignited green and reached the red

ODOM

faceplate on the helmet, Jack had his water lights of red/green. When the voice from the tower sounded in his ears and bounced around too unintelligently inside his skull and helmet, Jack had his MC. There was the sound of a roulette wheel spinning in Jack's head and with every click the scene he was picturing flashed from the cockpit to the water tank, cockpit to water tank. As the clicking became further apart, the scenes began to slow down, slow motion—cockpit to water tank, cockpit to water tank.

As the rocket fired and shook volcanically, Jack could feel the shackles slipping from his body. He could feel them falling around his feet and clanging at the bottom of the tank, reverberating and sending clusters of bubbles racing to the top, past his head, where they popped themselves against the heavy, steel lid that had been slammed shut over the top of him.

"Minus 56"

Jack pressed his feet flat against the floor of the water chamber and gripped the chain that was connecting him to the octagonal bottom with tight fists. Veins bulged against the skin in his neck and forearms and his lungs burned with the lack of oxygen. He didn't have much left—time, that is, in any respect. He was putting together his last attempts at pulling himself out of this one.

The other chains were lying like snakes at the bottom of the tank—the wrist shackles and the ones for the ankles and waist. They moved in the water as Jack repositioned his feet, clinking together, but the only one of any consequence was gripping Jack around his throat and trying to kill him. It was taut and straining under continuous effort. It was giving. He was giving.

Jack renegotiated with his lungs in an attempt to buy some more time, but they were ready for the water. There was a little voice inside Jack's internal engine that reminded him that water contains one-third oxygen and marine animals live very well in that sort of environment. But Jack, for the time being, held dominion over his body and continued to tug.

He could sense the tension outside the tank like it was going to collapse it. He expected to see the glass shatter and spill him out onto the stage in front of all those people. He decided he'd play dead if that should happen. He'd made that decision. To hell with those people and their bullshit sympathy, he thought. He'd just roll over and give them some of what they wanted—a

ODOM

little death. Then he would come back again, same time next year. But the glass wasn't shattering or collapsing and Jack stayed on that chain, laying into it with the last of his energy. It was giving. He was giving. He squatted down closer to the bottom and really put the last of his legs into it and the chain started to come loose. A metallic pop sounded through the water. Jack floated toward the top and pushed at the steel lid. He popped it open and bathed in the red stage lights that awaited him—took in great breaths and heavy applause from the gallery.

# # #

Jack hung over the side of the water chamber and refilled himself with oxygen. His senses came back to center again. His strength accompanied them. It was good to be alive, Jack thought. He heard the applause and he felt the flashing camera bulbs on his skin, but he couldn't see anything because of the lights. There were spotlights, TV lights that were coming from the front of the stage as well as the balcony, and the camera flashes. They made it seem that everything was still in slow motion—still, as it had been under the water.

"Way to go, Jack, you goddam son–of–a–bitch. You did it! You did it you goddam motherfucker," said Buddy. He was screaming and kneeling next to Jack, slapping him on his back and laughing. "You goddam motherfucker."

The stage hands backed the volunteers away from the tank, away from Buddy, and the Armand Lyle backed away and plastered a smile across his face, raised his hands to the applauding audience. A doctor approached Jack and Buddy.

"Are you OK?" the doctor asked Jack.

Jack raised his hand out of the water and gave him the thumbs up. "I'm fine," he said.

"Goddam motherfucker," Buddy said, laughing and slapping Jack on the back.

# # #

The stagehands helped Jack out of the tank and quickly got him out of the neck manacle and into his "Suicide Simmons" robe. The crowd applauded loudly and appreciatively, standing, but Jack considered it

nothing more than a knee–jerk. He'd popped out of the tank and they'd popped out of their seats. It was all in the program.

As the MC rambled on about bravery and danger as he had at the beginning, Jack wanted to snatch his microphone away from him. He wanted to grab Armand Lyle by his necktie, raise him into the air high above the crowd, and scream into the microphone "Brawn over brains!" He wanted to use that adrenaline. He wanted to let loose that vulgarity. "Brawn over brains!"

But he didn't. In the end he filled his ego with accolades as he had his lungs with oxygen, and pushed a smile onto his lips as Buddy had requested. The countdown to the new beginning was ending, and as the new year dawned and the orgasm at countdown's end was disintegrating into an unintelligible hum, the focus shifted from Jack and his brilliant feats to the most recent, annual celebration of drinking and laughing.

Jack, the last to leave the platform via the back steps, made his way through handshakes to the front of the stage. He took a last glance at the tank of water. The curtain had been pulled back after he had emerged, and it was still in the lights and calm like it had been the first time he'd looked at it. He rubbed his eyes for a minute and took a last look, took a deep breath and turned himself toward the crowd again. It was focusing on celebration; some of it was leaving. It was humming all over with satisfaction.

Jack felt pretty good, too. He felt clean for awhile. But

ODOM

as his final act of the evening, he turned his back on all the lights and all that satisfaction, and tried to find the quickest way out of the place.

It was too goddamn much.

MINUS 55

The author, Andrew Odom

    Andrew Odom, who describes himself as "sensationally gorgeous," currently lives in Evansville, Indiana, working diligently on his next book, *On the Verge*. He was born sometime this century, in some American town, and grew up in Newburgh (also Indiana), where he primarily associated with his parents and older brother.
    Mr. Odom graduated with a degree in Journalism from the University of Southern Indiana, having begun his college experience by spending 3 years at Western Kentucky University. Such was his focus and diligence, that he crammed four years of college study into a mere six years.